There was no meal for Jessie tonight. She grew tired of barking and lay down with her head on her paws. She no longer bothered to listen for Matt. She hadn't given up hope. She would never do that. There just didn't seem to be any point in listening anymore.

Come Home
JESSIE

by Christine Pullein-Thompson

Cover illustration by Doug Henry

Published by Willowisp Press, Inc.
10100 SBF Drive, Pinellas Park, Florida 34666

Copyright© 1991 by Christine Pullein-Thompson

Printed in the United States of America

10 9 8 7 6 5 4 3 2 1

ISBN 0-87406-561-5

One

"WE must take Jessie along. Look, she's waiting," cried Matt.

"But it's going to be very hot later," said Lucy Painter, Matt's mother. She looked at the cloudless sky. "I hate to leave Jessie alone in the hot car while we shop. I also have other errands to run while we're out."

"But I don't need to be with you the whole time," said Matt. "After we've shopped, I'll take her for a run in the park while you finish up your errands. We can meet back at the car," insisted Matt.

"I suppose that would be all right," said Mrs. Painter with a sigh.

Jessie was watching them. Then, as if she understood what they were saying, she went ahead and waited by the car while Mrs. Painter searched for the car keys. Jessie waited patiently, watching the chickens scratch in the flower beds.

Another summer had come to Willow Tree Farm. Grass throughout the English countryside was emerald green. The trees were heavy with leaves and the walkways were brightly bordered with flowers.

"I'll get a dish and a bottle of water. You'll be all right in the car, won't you Jessie?" Matt asked. And Jessie, a black Labrador, wagged her tail happily.

Jasper, Jessie's son, was locked in the barn. Matt would take him out later. Jasper couldn't be trusted in the car alone. He was capable of tearing at the upholstery with his teeth, and would bark wildly at passersby. Matt liked Jasper, but he didn't love him as much as Jessie. Jasper lacked Jessie's gentle nature and was always wanting something—a walk, another walk, more food, a ball game. He was tireless and demanding, and never really satisfied.

Mrs. Painter backed the brand new Volvo station wagon slowly and carefully out of the garage. She had only driven it once before.

Jessie was in the cargo part of the car, separated from the passenger seats by a plastic partition. She was unhappy. She had always traveled on the seats in the old car. Now she felt caged like a wild animal. Matt knew how she felt, but his father had insisted that the dogs stay off the seats of his new car.

"I don't want it covered with dog hair when I'm entertaining clients," he had said. "I'm sorry, but that's the way it is." Matt understood how his father felt. The car was his father's pride and joy, the best he had ever owned.

Matt wished his father was home instead of temporarily working in Holland, returning only for weekends. His mother was usually busy, too, running a shop with her friend, Candy. It wasn't an ordinary shop. It wasn't even an antique shop, though it sold old things such as copper pans, fire grates, and antique china. Called "Just Your Luck," the shop tried to find customers what they wanted, which meant that Matt's mother was always searching for things like ancient books and brass fenders. Matt often helped, but today he didn't feel like it. There was a park near the shopping center, and he planned to lie there with Jessie and just watch the ducks on the pond.

Turning onto the main road, Mrs. Painter said, "I've got to stop at the bank, and I've got to find you some new shoes. Then I've got to find a copper preserving pan, a second-hand sewing machine, and an old-fashioned brass door knocker. You'll have to hang around a while, Matt. I'm sorry. And I have to go straight to the shop afterward, so it's going to be a lot of waiting."

In the back of the car, Jessie panted. She hated going to the shop as much as Matt did. She loved Willow Tree Farm and would be happy to spend all of her time there.

"I told you I don't mind," Matt said. "After we do the banking and get my shoes, I'll sit in the park while you're at the shop with Candy. Jessie loves the park. It's a nice change for her."

Mrs. Painter eased the car into a space in the shopping center's parking lot. "All right, but let's hurry now," she said. "I've got to be at the shop by twelve, otherwise Candy will have my hide," she continued, unbuckling her seat belt.

The parking lot was full of people and shopping carts. Ignoring his mother, Matt wound down the back windows and said, "We won't be long, Jessie, I promise. Just five minutes."

7

Jessie was panting already when Mrs. Painter said, "I've got to go to the bank first. We can't be long. You can be prosecuted for leaving a dog in a car in this weather. And it's going to be a scorcher."

Then she hurried ahead, her mind full of things that she needed to get for customers. As far as Matt was concerned, none of them were half as important as Jessie. Why couldn't his mother stay at home like his friends' mothers? Martin's mother aways seemed to be home, making delicious things like sponge cake and pudding.

When they reached the bank, Mrs. Painter took a place in line and as they stood waiting for a cashier, she turned to Matt and whispered, "It's just one of those days, I guess."

Matt didn't answer. He was already worrying about Jessie, hot and alone in the car. And after the bank, he pretended to like the shoes his mother pointed out at the third store they'd visited. He just wanted to stop shopping and get back to the car.

"Take them with you and go ahead," said Mrs. Painter. "I'll have plenty to carry in a minute. I'm just going to the market. I'll be as quick as I can, I promise. Oh, wait a minute, I'll give you some money for an ice cream cone. Hang on."

"I don't care about an ice cream cone, Mom. I'm going to give Jessie some water. It's been nearly an hour since we left the car. Look at the clock on the town hall!"

Matt began to run down the hot street toward the parking lot, imagining Jessie's welcome and her delight at seeing him. She would leap out of the car wagging her tail, her eyes saying, "Where now?"

"You didn't lock it, did you?" Matt shouted over his shoulder.

"No," his mother called back.

As Matt went toward the parking lot, he noticed a plane in the sky, and a large lady feeding the ducks on the pond. *Poor Jessie*, he thought. *Mom was right. It's going to be a scorcher.*

*　*　*　*　*

Jessie lay with her head on her paws. She hated the new car. It didn't smell of anything she could recognize and the floor in the cargo area was hard compared to the seat she had had in the old car. There was nothing to see, either, besides people rushing here and there, pushing their shopping carts. She had hoped they were going somewhere exciting when she had gotten into the car.

Soon Jessie was panting, and when someone tapped on the window to say, "Oh you poor thing, are you thirsty?" she growled in reply. At that moment, she didn't feel like being pleasant to anyone. After a time, she sat up watching for Matt and his mother to return. Jessie's tongue was hanging out and the small white patch beneath her chin gleamed against her shiny black coat. She wasn't really thinking of anything, just waiting. To her, the day seemed just like any other day—only hotter and duller. And now she wanted only two things—Matt and a long drink of cold water.

*　*　*　*　*

9

The three men had tried to break into five cars by the time they reached the Volvo. The tallest, who was called Darron, opened the driver's door and then whistled to the other two. "We've found what we want, get in! They've even left the keys in the ignition. This is perfect for the robbery and getaway! Come on, hurry. We need to look as though we own it, for heaven's sake," he muttered.

Jessie growled from the back.

"What about the dog?" asked Tony, one of Darron's partners.

"Get in," Darron said. "There's no time to waste. We'll worry about the dog later." He settled behind the steering wheel, and watched his partners hurry into the car behind him.

Darron was tall, dark-haired, and wore one earring. Tony was slim with neat hands. Another partner, Carl, was huge, with coarse features. He was as strong as the other two put together.

Tony could pick locks, and Carl could batter down a door, but Darron was the boss.

Jessie started to bark and claw at the partition that separated her from the three robbers. Carl scowled at the dog.

A small girl passing by stared at Jessie, then tugged at her mother's arm. "Mom, Mom, look at the doggy!" she said. But the girl's mother replied, "Oh, please be quiet, Natalie. I haven't got time to look at anything." She hurried off, dragging the little girl with her.

Darron let out his breath. "We've got a lot of distance to cover," he told the others. "And we don't want to arrive too early. So you two can sit back and relax. I'll tell you when you can get your masks out. But just remember, there's to be no violence, Carl. We are not in the business of beating up old ladies. That's kids' stuff."

Jessie had stopped barking and sat with her nose pressed against the partition. Her lips were drawn back in a snarl. She could smell the three men. They smelled of sweaty clothes, cigarettes, and unwashed bodies. She knew she should be with Matt, not here with three strange men. But there was nothing she could do except wait for a chance to get away.

If Jasper had been there he would have tried to tear the partition down with his teeth, but Jessie had teeth bred to carry dead game without damaging it. Hers were not killer teeth, and she wasn't a fighter by nature. So Jessie could only wait for her chance at escape—if it came at all.

* * * * *

When Matt reached the parking lot he was very hot, and still hating the new canvas shoes he carried. He thought, *Martin will laugh at them and call them girls' shoes.* But they weren't girls' shoes. They were what the sales clerk called 'unisex' shoes. Matt wished now that he had refused to get them. But his mother had insisted that he get new shoes.

And Matt, already worrying about Jessie, had agreed, and then stood stamping his feet with impatience while the sales clerk wrapped the shoes. He wanted to shout when his mother paid for them. It seemed as if she counted each coin twice before giving it to the clerk.

11

By then, Matt was sick with worry over Jessie and he *still* had to buy his father the *TV Times*. Matt was twelve now, and he had made a promise to get the television guide, and his father expected promises to be kept. But keeping the promise had delayed things further. There was a line in the shop where Matt went to buy the *TV Times*. Old ladies ahead of Matt fumbled with their money, and then a child argued over the price of a bag of candy. She left in tears, just a few pennies short of what she needed.

Imagine crying over a bag of candy, Matt thought, shuffling his feet impatiently. But then, when his turn came, he dropped his money all over the floor and had the humiliation of grabbing for it among people's feet. His eyes flooded with tears of frustration as other customers sighed and muttered. But at last he was outside again in the burning heat, running through the parking lot.

There was a long line of cars waiting for a space, and a sea of people with shopping carts. And then Matt couldn't see the car. He was certain they had left it in a space by the shopping center wall, but it wasn't there. An orange car was parked in its place, with maps on the backseat and a man's cap in the front. *I can't be wrong. I know we left the car there,* Matt kept thinking. But a sense of panic was rising inside him, making him want to scream. *I must be mistaken,* he decided, knowing deep down inside that he wasn't.

He searched the endless lines of cars and even spotted an identical one. But the rush of hope was dashed a moment later when he saw that the car had different upholstery and no Jessie.

He ran up and down the lines of cars once more like a madman, his heart throbbing wildly. Next, he stopped a man to ask, "Have you seen a dark blue Volvo here with a Labrador in the back?"

The man, whose stomach hung over his trousers, looked at Matt as though he were crazy, and snapped, "I don't have time to go around looking at cars. What's a dog doing in one in this heat, anyway? That's what I would like to know."

Then Matt wondered whether his mother could have arrived at the parking lot first, and driven home without him. But that didn't make sense. His mother had been going in the other direction. And anyway, she would never forget him.

The sweat was streaming off Matt's face and he thought, *I'm going crazy! The car must be somewhere!* But it wasn't there, not the car, nor a single sign of Jessie.

Matt ran back up the main street, looking for his mother. He wanted to stop everyone he passed and ask, "Have you seen a dark blue Volvo station wagon with a black Labrador in the back?" But he knew it would be useless because no one would have seen anything. They would be thinking of the price of meat and vegetables, and what they were going to buy. And now he hated the people walking down the street, staring into shop windows. They all seemed so large and fat, and stupid, and slow...oh, so slow. They blocked his way and wouldn't hurry. Looking for his mother, he felt like a mouse trying to force its way through a herd of elephants.

He found her at last in a store, haggling over the

price of a brass door knocker. "The car's gone and Jessie's gone!" Matt cried. He burst into tears.

His mother handed the store clerk a handful of coins. She turned to Matt to say, "You must have made a mistake. The car can't be gone."

"But it's not there. I've looked and looked!" shouted Matt.

They ran out of the store and down the street together, banging into people as they went. They didn't speak, because suddenly it was too bad for words. Mrs. Painter went straight to the shopping center wall. "We left it here, didn't we?" she asked, and Matt nodded.

"I didn't leave the key in the ignition, did I?" she asked. She fumbled in her bag for the key, then gave up the search as a lost cause.

Matt said nothing, for he could not bear to blame his mother. It was his fault, too. He should have noticed. Martin would have noticed if he'd been there. He would have said, "Don't forget your key, Mrs. Painter," his small face smiling as he spoke. Although Martin tended to do poorly in school, he wasn't a fool. Another of Matt's close friends, Anne, would also have noticed. She would have made a joke of it, because Anne made a joke of nearly everything.

But Matt *hadn't* noticed, so it was his fault, too.

"We had better go to the police, Matt. Do you know where the police station is?" asked Mrs. Painter.

Matt shook his head. He felt numb with fear. And even though it was boiling hot outside, he felt cold inside. His mother had turned pale and was shivering. "We'll ask. Come on, we can't stand here like zombies," she cried. "The sooner we do something,

14

the sooner we'll get them back."

And Matt knew they were both thinking the same thing. It wasn't just Jessie who mattered. The car mattered, too. It was the apple of Matt's father's eye. Maurice Painter had saved for it and had gone without all sorts of things to pay for it. They had only had it a week, and now it was gone. Although it was insured, Mr. Painter would still be upset, and who could blame him?

"Things will turn out all right," Matt's mother said, trying to comfort him. But Matt was beyond comfort. *We can get another car exactly the same, but there will never be another Jessie,* he thought. He was seeing his life without her stretching ahead like a desert. And all because of their stupidity. If they had locked the car and taken the key with them, they would be driving home now with Jessie in the back.

"Where do you think Jessie is now?" Matt asked, following his mother.

"I don't know. I just wish I did," his mother answered. She stopped a woman and asked for directions, then said to Matt, "Come on, the police station is by the library and there's no time to lose."

"I hate the shoes we got me, Mom. I'll never wear them now!" shouted Matt. He ran after her. "If we hadn't taken so long finding them I might have been in time to save Jessie and the car, because no one would have stolen it with me there, would they, Mom? I would have screamed and screamed..."

But Matt's mother didn't answer. She just hurried on with her head bent, her arms loaded with packages from the stores.

Two

DARRON drove steadily, taking no chances. He didn't want to be noticed and, because of that, was dressed soberly in a striped shirt, trousers, and lace-up shoes. The other two men wore sweatshirts and jeans. They were all on edge. They had to be if they were to succeed. They were afraid, too, because things might go wrong.

Jessie could smell their fear and was uneasy.

Tony tried to make friends with the dog, talking to her through the plastic partition, calling her "a good dog." But Jessie would have nothing to do with him and merely looked the other way.

After a while, Tony asked, "How much further is it?"

And Darron, who was driving more slowly now, said, "Only seven miles. We don't want to get there before the place is closed for the lunch break. Try to look normal in the meantime."

Darron's eyes darted left and right. "And don't leave anything behind," he continued. "We don't want the detectives to find anything useful when they find this car."

Carl lit a cigarette. "We could ditch it," he said. "We could push it in a river."

"But what about the dog?" Tony asked.

"Ditch her with the car, right into a river, that's what I think," Carl said with a grunt. I'll take care of it—one way or another."

Tony looked at Carl's hard eyes. "It should be something gentle...maybe she doesn't have to die at all."

"Oh, yeah?" asked Carl. "Just supposing she barks and gives the game away? Whoever owns the car has probably reported it *and* the dog missing by now. So the dog's a liability whichever way you look at it. She has to go, and it's really no big deal to see that she goes permanently."

Carl smiled wickedly. "No big deal at all."

* * * * *

"What make of car?" the policeman asked Mrs. Painter.

The police station was smaller than Matt had expected and less formal. There was a woman working a vacuum cleaner in the background and an empty coffee mug on the counter. Matt was calmer now and desperately trying to accept that Jessie had gone and might never return.

"Can I have the license plate number, please?" the policeman asked next.

"I don't know. I can't remember, but the car itself is dark blue and brand new. That's what makes it all so much worse," replied Mrs. Painter.

The policeman suppressed a sigh.

"And there's a black Labrador in the back," added Matt, not for the first time. "But she isn't absolutely black. She's got a small streak of white under her chin. They may have thrown her out of the car. She may be on a highway by now. She could be dead. But whatever's happened, we want her back!" he finished.

"Address? Your address, please." The policeman sounded fed up with them. It was obvious that he had never been stupid enough to leave a car unlocked with the key in the ignition, a brand new car, too, and it was probably something he would talk about for the rest of the day.

Or maybe the policeman was just bored by the whole business. He wrote down the Painters' address. Then he asked whether it might be possible to speak to Mr. Painter.

"Sorry, he's away in Holland," replied Mrs. Painter. "He's working there," she continued, nearly adding, "And he'll be very upset."

"Wait here, then, and I will get Officer Flatman to run you home," the policeman said.

"I imagine you have the car documents there?" he asked with a condescending smile.

Matt's mother nodded, and imagined her customer waiting for the door knocker at "Just Your Luck," fuming, no doubt. Mrs. Painter knew her partner, Candy, would be fuming, too.

Officer Flatman had a happy smile, which showed off perfect teeth. He held the police car door open for them, while the first policeman told him where to go—as though Matt and his mother were incapable of doing anything for themselves. He also asked about Jessie. "I had a Labrador myself once. Wonderful dogs, aren't they?" he added, starting the engine.

"The best," said Matt, who had never ridden in a police car before and might have enjoyed the ride if he hadn't been worrying about Jessie.

Officer Flatman turned to smile at Matt and say, "Don't worry, we'll find her. As soon as we've got the number of the car, we'll be flashing it to all the police cars on duty. And we won't forget the dog. What's she called?"

"Jessie," said Matt. "And she's the best dog a person could have."

Willow Tree Farm was looking beautiful when they reached it. The roses were out and everywhere the grass was bright green. Ducks swam with their ducklings on the pond where once Jessie had almost drowned beneath the ice. Elijah, their goat, was tied up by the barn. And the handyman, old Will, was sitting by the back door, waiting to be paid. Everything looked so wonderful it made Matt feel like crying again.

Will stared at them with dismay, but was too tactful to ask what had happened. Matt saw Will's old eyes looking for Jessie, then darting back to Officer Flatman. Probably, Will was imagining they had been in a crash.

"The car's been stolen, Will. Jessie was inside," explained Mrs. Painter.

"Poor old Jessie," was all Will said, though Jessie wasn't old at all yet.

They all went indoors together. Before looking up the car's license plate number and registration documents, Matt's mother put the tea kettle on the stove, as she always did automatically. Hearing the police car, Jasper had started to bark in the barn.

"Jessie was yours, was she?" asked Officer Flatman kindly, smiling at Matt.

"That's right." Matt couldn't bear to talk about it now, not to anyone.

Officer Flatman stayed to drink a cup of coffee, then he stood to leave with the information about the car. But before going, he told Matt, "Don't worry. The people who took the car and your dog are probably a bunch of joyriders who will abandon the car as soon as it runs out of gas."

Matt knew Officer Flatman was only being kind, because joyriders steal cars in the evening, not in broad daylight from shopping center parking lots. Even Matt knew that.

His mother was on the telephone now apologizing to her partner, saying, "The door knocker's here, but I don't have a car."

Matt looked outside at the sunshine and it seemed to mock him. His mother paid Will, then said to Matt, "We had better call your father next. Do you want to talk to him, Matt?"

"If there's time," Matt said.

It was nearly lunchtime now. The next day, his best friend, Anne, was to arrive for a week's vacation with them. Matt had been looking forward to it, but now he didn't care. The only thing that mattered was Jessie. She was lost somewhere, perhaps trying to get home.

"I expect your father will be angry," said Mrs. Painter. "How I hate new things. Something always happens to them."

But Mr. Painter took them both by surprise. He sounded calm and said, "Don't worry about the car. It's Jessie who matters. We can always get another car. Call the insurance company right away. Rent another car and I will be home as soon as I can. I've got to go to a working lunch now, but I'll be thinking of you all the time. I'll call this evening as soon as I can. I'm so sorry."

Matt grabbed the receiver. "Come back soon Dad, please," he cried. "We must find Jessie. Where do you think she is?"

"I don't know, but we'll find her," said Mr. Painter. "Look after your mother, Matt. I must go now. I'm late already. Be brave."

Matt put down the receiver slowly and turned to his mother. "He says we'll find her, but I don't see how," he said.

*　*　*　*　*

Jessie looked out of the back window. They were in the country now. Darron turned the car down a narrow lane and Jessie could smell sheep and cows through the open windows.

"Only another minute and we'll be at the post office," Darron said, looking at his watch. "Get your masks and gloves ready. And don't forget the bags."

Darron had his own iron bar to use as a threat, but he wouldn't let the others use it. "You might go too far," he told them. "And we don't want anyone murdered. Remember, the woman on duty at the post office is an old lady who could be your granny.

21

Treat her kindly."

"I haven't got a grandmother, and supposing there's a customer inside?" said Carl. "And she won't open the safe if we're kind. You know how tough old ladies can be."

"There won't be a customer," Tony reminded Carl. "It's lunchtime."

They were all tense now, and Jessie could smell their fear again.

"What about the dog? Where should we put the money?" asked Carl.

"On the backseat," Darron replied. "If we pull her out now people will notice, and anyway, we haven't got time."

The post office took up the front portion of an old cottage. It was run by an elderly lady. In addition to postage stamps, it sold candy and items such as hair barrettes, safety pins, envelopes, and writing paper.

The men put on their gloves and slid the masks over their faces, then ran toward the cottage. A sign that said "Closed Til 2:00 p.m." hung from a small window. The post office door was locked, but easily gave way against Carl's weight.

Sensing that something was wrong, Jessie started barking wildly and scratching at the Volvo's rear window. Some passing children noticed her. And an old man on a bicycle saw the car. But Jessie and the car looked respectable enough, and the old man thought Jessie was just tired of waiting in the heat.

Except for Jessie's constant barking, everything was quiet. Not a sound came from the post office. And there was nothing in the car to give the robbers away—no gloves, no mask, no guns. Everything looked ordinary. The Volvo, parked sensibly outside the tiny country post office, could have belonged to a doctor, a salesman—anybody.

The three robbers worked swiftly. A tiny, old woman in a faded summer dress and open-toed sandals was eating her lunch when they burst in.

"We won't hurt you if you keep quiet," Darron said, smiling at her. "We just want the keys and the money."

She didn't fight back. She just told them that the keys were in a box in the sitting room and that they were welcome to the money. They picked up a few odds and ends for good measure. Carl took the old woman's necklace as well, undoing it with large, clumsy hands, breaking the clasp as he did so. They left her tied to a chair—not too tightly—because they didn't want her to be there too long. Finally, Carl found her handbag and took the wallet from inside. It was stuffed with cash.

Then they said, "So long, thanks for now," just as though she had invited them in. As soon as they were out the door they removed their masks and gloves. They hurried toward the car, carrying the two bags they had brought with them, stuffed now with money. As they got back into the car, they were calm and quiet, and looked quite ordinary again.

"It was a picnic, wasn't it? She didn't even scream," Darron said as he started the engine.

"If only they were all like that," replied Carl, while Jessie snarled helplessly from the back.

In the cottage, the old woman struggled to free herself, while at Willow Tree Farm, Matt and his mother were trying to enjoy their lunch. Meanwhile, the police had started circulating a full description of the dark blue Volvo with a black Labrador in the back.

Soon Darron said, "Just down this lane and we've almost made it. Peter should be waiting for us. I hope he is, because this car will be on the wanted list soon, and we don't want to be around when it is."

Tall trees cast shadows in the lane. At the end of it stood a small cottage used by its owners only on weekends.

Darron eased the big Volvo into the garage nearby. At the same moment, a red car slid into view.

"Perfect, absolutely perfect timing," said Darron. "Now don't leave anything behind, except the dog, of course."

"Shouldn't we do her in?" asked Carl. "She could recognize us and put us in jail. Dogs never forget, do they? If you'll let me have your tire iron, Darron, I'll finish her off. It won't take a minute. She won't even howl."

Darron seemed to be thinking it over.

"There won't be any blood. There won't be a sign. It'll be quick," Carl assured him.

And Tony, speaking for the first time since the robbery, said, "Better to get rid of her Carl's way, Darron. She'll howl if we leave her here and, if we turn her loose, she'll lead the police to the car. I don't like the idea, either, but we can't risk just letting her go, Darron."

Peter, their fourth partner, was tooting his horn now.

But Darron's grandmother had a dog and it always

24

welcomed him. He remembered how it sat by the fire, keeping his grandmother company.

"I don't want her killed," said Darron at last. "I like dogs."

"We can't risk letting her go," insisted Carl.

"He's right," said Tony. "Let's just get it over with."

"She hasn't done us any harm," replied Darron.

"But she will," Carl insisted. "You just wait and see."

Three

JASPER was howling.

"I'll take him to see Martin. I won't be long," Matt told his mother.

When he let Jasper out of the barn, the big black-and-tan dog stood looking for Jessie. "She's gone, Jasper," Matt said. "Jessie's gone. We may never see her again." Putting it into words made it sound that much worse, and somehow horribly final. And Jasper seemed to understand, for he stopped looking for Jessie and nuzzled Matt's hand with his nose.

"We're going to see Martin. We must tell him. We must tell everybody," Matt said. He clipped Jasper's leash onto his studded collar.

They took a shortcut, running and walking in turns. Martin, one of Matt's best friends, lived with his parents in a cottage in the only wooded area for miles. His father was a gamekeeper who worked for Lord Hislop. As gamekeeper, he mostly raised pheasants for the hunters who came every autumn—rich people who paid hundreds of dollars for the pleasure of the hunt. Matt couldn't understand it. His father called it "business." His mother said, "That's life." But Matt thought it was more like death than life, and tried not to think about it at all. Now, however, as he entered the woods, he wondered how Martin could bear it. There were pheasants everywhere, lurking in the high hedges nearby, crouching in long grass, eating corn on a track that wound through the woods. Everything was remote and beautiful here.

When Matt knocked on the cottage door, Martin's mother opened it. She was wearing jeans, a checkered shirt, and sneakers. She glanced at Matt and Jasper and said, "You look like you're falling to pieces, Matt. Where's Jessie?"

"Gone," replied Matt. He tugged on Jasper's leash, and wandered with the dog into the small, cluttered sitting room where Martin was watching television. His friend had a bag of potato chips in one hand and a can of cola in the other. Jasper's big tail knocked a knickknack off a table when he lunged toward a cat leaping through an open window.

"Jessie's gone," Matt repeated, bending down to pick up the knickknack, which was a pheasant made of china.

"What! Did she run away?" asked Martin. His voice sounded interested, but his eyes remained glued to the TV show in which cowboys were battling Indians.

"Run away?" cried Matt. "Don't be stupid. Jessie wouldn't run away. She's been stolen with Dad's new car."

"Oh, dear, oh, dear, I am sorry," said Martin's mother. "I really am. Poor old Jessie!"

"What does your Dad think? It was a brand new

car, wasn't it? You only had it a week," Martin said, looking at Matt at last.

"He thinks Jessie is far more important," replied Matt. "He doesn't mind about a car, because you can buy a new car any time, but he thinks Jessie's different—Jessie can't be replaced." Matt was suddenly proud of his father.

"That's true," said Martin's mother, opening a package of cookies and holding it out to Matt.

"Have you told the police?" asked Martin, his eyes returning to the TV screen.

Matt felt disheartened. "Yes, of course. We're not complete idiots."

And he thought that Martin just didn't seem to care. Matt wondered if living in a place where pheasants were raised just to be shot gave his friend a different view of life. Still, Matt had always thought Martin was fond of Jessie and it upset him that Martin appeared more interested in TV than in real life. But then, seeming to read his thoughts, Martin jumped up and switched off the TV.

"Come on," Martin said. "We'll search the woods. Just let me get my shoes."

"But she won't be in these woods," said Matt. "She would be nearly home if she was. She's miles away by now, probably still locked in the car. If she was free she would come straight home. I know she would."

"What did the police say, then?" asked Martin. He pushed potato chips into his mouth.

"Not a lot," Matt answered.

Jasper was whining and straining at his leash. He hated the small room and wanted to be outside again.

"How did you get home if the car was stolen?" asked

Martin.

"A policeman named Officer Flatman drove us there," replied Matt, walking toward the back door with Jasper.

"I'll ask Dad to keep an eye open for Jessie. He gets out a lot. We can ask people," Martin said. But Matt had the feeling that all Martin really wanted now was to get back to the television set, that he wouldn't care about anything else until the show was over.

"She won't be near here. How many more times do I have to tell you?" shouted Matt. "She may be anywhere—on the highway, or dead for all we know!"

"All dog pounds and breeders should be contacted," advised Martin's mother. She still carried the cookie package. She offered the package to Matt again, saying, "Here take one. Cheer up. All is not lost." Matt shook his head. *As though cookies could heal one's misery,* he thought.

Matt hurried out past the hunting dogs kept in pens. The dogs looked at him hopefully.

When Matt reached home again he found a strange car in the drive. "Thank goodness you're back," said his mother, rushing out of the house to greet him. "I've got to go to the shop. What do you think of the car? It's been loaned to me by Bill Abbott, the landlord of the White Horse restaurant. Isn't he kind?"

His mother had changed into a different dress and had done her hair. Matt glared at her. He wanted her to be concerned only for Jessie, nothing else. So he didn't speak. He just took Jasper indoors with him, keeping his eyes on the ground.

His mother called after him, "I'll only be 10

minutes. Please don't let Jasper get on the sofa."

Matt tied Jasper to a chair while he called the animal rescue service. But no one there had news of Jessie.

"Call the police," suggested the voice at the other end when Matt explained what had happened.

"We have," Matt said.

"Keep in touch then. We'll inform headquarters and let you know if she turns up anywhere."

After that Matt spent five minutes chewing his nails until there was nothing left to chew. Then, untying Jasper, he went with him along the driveway to the road and waited there for a miracle to happen, even though it was too much to hope for. Jessie wasn't going to find her way home. Even so, Matt kept imagining her arriving home dusty and footsore, her head down. And he pictured the slow, guilty wag of her tail when she saw him, because Jessie always blamed herself for whatever went wrong.

Jasper hated waiting on the road. He yawned, showing a mouthful of healthy young teeth. Then he whined, and looked up at Matt, his tongue hanging out. His amber eyes seemed to say, "What next? Aren't we going anywhere? What's the point of standing in the road? Can't we do something?"

But Matt had no idea of what else they could do now to find Jessie. After a while he returned to Willow Tree Farm and untied Elijah, the white goat they had been given nearly a year ago. He put Elijah in the barn and gave him water, half of which Jasper drank. The bucket had to be filled again, and as Matt did that, he thought, *Suppose Jessie's still in the car without water? How long does it take a dog to die of thirst?*

Then Matt fed the chickens, which had once belonged to the previous owners of the farm. Jasper watched. Once, he might have killed them. Now he knew that they belonged to Matt and must not be touched.

When his chores were finished, Matt sat on the garden seat and stared at the lawn. But he wasn't really seeing the lawn. He was picturing his father packing his suitcase in Holland. Matt could hardly wait for his father's return. *He'll know what to do,* he thought. *He always does.*

Soon Matt's mother returned in the borrowed car. "Any news, love?" she asked.

Matt shook his head. "What are we going to do now, Mom? We can't just sit here and wait for something to happen."

"We'll have a cup of tea. Then we'll drive around and have a look. Cheer up, love. It's early in the day yet," she said, going into the house, taking off her shoes, and putting the kettle on to boil.

That's my mother, thought Matt as he followed her into the kitchen. *She's always looking on the bright side when things are blackest. Or is she just trying to cheer me up?*

Later, they set out to search for Jessie. It was cooler now, with a haze settling over the open fields. Mrs. Painter concentrated on handling the strange car. Matt looked for Jessie. But there wasn't a black Labrador anywhere. All Matt spotted were pedigree dogs being exercised by their owners, plus a few mongrels playing in the fields.

"Where do you think Jessie is?" asked Matt as they

drove toward home again.

"I don't know," his mother said. "I wish I did. But I expect she'll turn up. She's clever enough."

"It's like a bad dream, isn't it?" asked Matt.

"Yes, a nightmare—a really bad nightmare. Let's hope it'll end soon," she told him.

Then, after a while, Matt asked, "Do you think she could be in London, Mom? Because if she is, she might go to the apartment where she lived with Uncle Eric. Shall I call Anne when I get home? She'll check there for us. I know she will."

"It's a long shot," his mother replied as she steered the borrowed car back into the driveway at the farm. Her face was lined with worry. "You must realize we may never see Jessie again. Brace yourself for the possibility, Matt. And just remember that if it hadn't been for you and Anne, she would have drowned in that stream where you found her all those years ago. She was just a puppy."

Mom was right. It seemed a lifetime ago, that day he and Anne found Jessie tied in a sack and left to drown in the stream.

"I'll call Anne," he said, getting out of the car. "Then I'll take Jasper for a walk."

Anne was thunderstruck by Matt's news and kept crying, "Oh, Jessie, poor Jessie, she's so unlucky, so terribly unlucky."

"It was my fault. I wanted her to come with us. I wanted to take her for a run in the park," confessed Matt. "And now I feel so guilty."

"Don't be silly, Matt!" insisted Anne. "It's fate. It has nothing to do with you."

"Yes, but if only we had locked the car doors and

taken the keys," explained Matt.

"If, if, if...it's no good thinking of ifs," replied Anne, who was about two years older than Matt. "It's negative. You've got to be positive, that's what Gran says."

"I suppose," said Matt.

"And anyway," continued Anne, "I'll go straight over to your Uncle Eric's old apartment. I'll take a double-decker bus and ride up top so I can see Jessie if she's wandering the streets on her own. That way I won't miss her. I'll also leave my name and address if someone new is living in the apartment by now. Don't worry, Matt, we'll find her! I'm coming to stay tomorrow—remember?"

That's Anne, thought Matt, putting down the receiver. *She never gives up, even though her parents hardly ever bother to see her and she has to live with her grandmother in London. Mom calls her a survivor and I think she's right. And all the animals love her, even cross old Elijah.*

Before Matt went to bed that night he called the police station once more, but there had been no news. Then his mother's friend, Candy, called to say that the Volvo had been used in a robbery.

"It was on the late local news. Didn't you watch it?" she shrieked. "An old man saw Jessie in the car. The gang got away with thousands, and Jessie was still alive then, so don't give up hope. The old man was on the TV news. So was the post mistress and *she's* all right. They only tied her up, thank goodness. So maybe they aren't vicious. Maybe they won't hurt Jessie."

Matt listened, hopping up and down with

33

excitement. *It's a lead at last!* he thought. *And while there's life, there's hope.*

Almost immediately after that, his father called and asked if there was any news. Matt told him what they'd heard. "I'll come home as soon as I can," his father promised again.

When Matt went to bed, he felt more hopeful. If Jessie was there when the post office was robbed, it meant that she hadn't been thrown out of the car, or killed right away.

Anne's words came back to Matt: "Be positive." He was going to be more positive from now on. *No more moaning,* he told himself, *only action.* And because the car thieves had taken part in a robbery, the police would be really searching for the blue Volvo now, and Matt regarded that as hopeful. He lay in bed imagining Jessie's return, and Jasper's excited welcome—the nightmare over.

* * * * *

As far as the robbers were concerned, Jessie was a nightmare. They had been arguing over the Labrador's fate since fleeing the scene of the robbery.

Peter, who had expected to be on the road moments after his three partners joined him, quickly had grown impatient.

"Forget about messing with her right now," he had said. "She'll die in this heat, anyway." Peter, who had long hair and a face pitted with acne, had grabbed a bag full of money. "Besides, there isn't time to bother. Just leave her in the Volvo and shut the garage doors. Come on. Let's go."

They left the garage, still muttering. Sweat was pouring off their faces as Tony slammed the garage doors shut. Hurriedly, they climbed into Peter's car. Jessie whined, then started to bark, trying to tell them to let her out, knowing it was her last chance.

"What did I tell you? She'll give us away," Carl hissed. "Someone will hear her. Some stupid woman on a horse will hear her and call the police. Look at the hoofprints in the lane. Horses go up and down here all the time. Any fool can see that!"

"There's no time," repeated Peter. He started up his car.

But now Jessie was barking with all her strength, and the sound echoed in the closed garage, drowning the sound of the car's engine. Carl cursed and leaped out of Peter's car. He opened the garage doors and found a spade. Then, pulling down the partition in the Volvo's cargo area, he waved the spade at Jessie, all the while yelling for the dog to shut up.

Jessie, feeling threatened, barked all the louder, and then she lunged. She wanted to get past him, but all Carl could see was the big Labrador coming at him, and he struck. He hit Jessie not once, but three times.

"Stupid beast!" he yelled, shaken. "See what you've made me do? Now try barking again. Go on, bark."

Darron pulled him away from the car. "That's enough. You've done enough," he said. "She's nothing but a poor, dumb animal, and you'll get us all in trouble."

"Well, what was I to do?" asked Carl. "She came straight at me. Would've bitten my head off. Besides, I've silenced her now, haven't I?" Carl followed Darron out of the garage and slammed the doors after him.

"Hurry!" called Peter. "We're on local radio. That old post office woman called the police already."

"I don't like it, Carl," said Tony as they drove away. "It'll be all over the papers: 'Vicious Gang Kills Dog.' There will be pictures of her. It'll be nearly as bad as killing the old lady. We'll have the animal protest groups after us. You don't think, do you, Carl? You don't use your brains. Sometimes I think you don't have any."

"Wasn't my fault," Carl muttered. "And besides, I've silenced her," he insisted. "She won't make trouble anymore."

* * * * *

Jessie lay on the backseat, her blood staining the Volvo's new upholstery. She was very thirsty now. There was water below her in a bottle with the dish Matt had left there, but even if she could reach it she would be unable to open the bottle.

Soon it was almost dark in the garage. Images came and went in Jessie's mind. They were fuzzy, and all from an almost-forgotten past, such as the time she'd waited by a roadside and barked to draw attention to a man named Eric who had been injured. Jessie remembered, too, how Will brought her goodies in his saddle bag, and she could almost see Jasper asking her to play. Still powerful was an image of Jessie's mate—Jasper's father—running with her in the moonlight. Jessie was barely conscious now, but the images continued floating before her eyes and once she thought she heard Matt calling, "Jessie, where are you?"

Later, Jessie dreamed. She dreamed she was running toward Matt, and that she licked his hand. All she wanted was to be at home with him again, the way things were supposed to be. But none of Jessie's body would move now when she asked it. Messages from her brain weren't getting through anymore. It was as though the main line of communication had been cut.

Finally, Jessie fell into a deeper, less painful sleep. But she was still bothered by nightmares in which she was chased by men across endless fields and couldn't find Matt. Her limbs twitched, and she whined and growled in her sleep. Hours later, light from another day filtered through the closed doors of the garage.

Four

ANNE waited for a bus outside her grandmother's house in Hampstead, London. As always, Matt's fair-haired friend wore a cheerful face, though in truth she was worried. Her mind kept straying to Jessie.

Poor Jessie, she's always in trouble, it seems. She must have been born under an unlucky star, she thought.

Anne could hardly bear waiting until she was in the country again at Matt's house, helping her friend search for Jessie. But first she had to go to the apartment where Jessie had once lived with Matt's Uncle Eric.

When the double-decker bus arrived, Anne climbed the stairs and sat in the front. She kept a lookout through the wide window for a black Labrador. But it was rush hour in London and all she could see were people and cars rushing this way and that, like swarming bees. They were all trying to get home as soon as possible. Tempers were fraying, and the sun was still burning down.

Anne changed buses. She thought it very unlikely

that the robbers would dump Jessie near London. But she wanted to be certain.

It's far more likely she's been dumped on a highway, she thought seconds later, *and is now dead. But I mustn't tell Matt that, not ever, because it would break his heart.*

When she reached the basement apartment that Uncle Eric used to live in, it was different from what she had expected. Matt had told her how run down it was. Now, she found it clean and freshly painted, and it had a new front door. She rang a bell and a young woman opened the door a few inches to look at her. The woman was holding a baby.

"Yes, what is it?" the woman asked. When Anne explained that she was hoping Jessie may have been spotted in the neighborhood, the woman said, "Definitely not. But if I do see the dog, I'll let the police know and they'll contact you."

Anne insisted that the woman jot down her grandmother's number. "We want Jessie back as soon as possible. She's a great dog."

Then Anne walked back down the street and caught a bus again, and then another bus. She never stopped looking for a tired, black Labrador, but she held out little hope. The streets were growing less busy now, and the sun was cooling. Another day was almost done.

After an unsuccessful search, Anne packed for her stay at Matt's house. She remembered to pack her boots and a thick sweater because the weather might change. She was trying not to think too much about Jessie, because if she did she would cry, and tears wouldn't bring Jessie back. Besides, her grandmother hated tears.

So instead, Anne thought of Willow Tree Farm as she packed. She thought of how quiet the farm was, and she thought of Elijah the goat. She thought of Jasper, whom she loved as much as Jessie, of his restless eyes and his sudden bouts of affection. He would put his paws on your shoulders and try to lick your face.

Anne decided that if she lived in the country permanently she would want a pony—or two, because a pony shouldn't live alone. *Then I would spend all my spare time riding,* she thought. But Matt didn't want a pony. He said that two dogs and a goat were enough. Of course, now there was only one dog. Anne knew Matt would be blaming himself, as he always did. He would keep saying that if he hadn't taken Jessie in the car, the trouble would never have happened. But Anne decided you could say that all the time about everything.

She went downstairs and helped her grandmother get supper. The sun was setting and the traffic was more quiet now, so quiet that Anne could hear voices in the street outside.

"I'll call you every day," Anne told her grandmother. And Gran's little dog, Kim, looked at Anne and knew she was going, for he had seen the suitcase being packed. He lay down with a sigh under the kitchen table, which was the coolest place in the apartment. Putting his nose on his paws, he watched Anne sadly.

*   *   *   *   *

Matt hardly slept that night. Trying to think positive didn't seem to work, and twice he went downstairs to open the back door and call, "Jessie, Jess, Jess, Jessie."

Frightened rabbits scuttled for their burrows at the sound of his voice and Jasper barked, but there was no Jessie. There was nothing but a countryside full of strange cries, which seemed to echo in the night. And there was a moon now, which made everything look silvery and magical.

The next time Matt opened the door to call, dawn was breaking and when he ran out in his bare feet, the grass was wet with dew. Mrs. Painter wasn't sleeping, either, and though it was only 5:00 in the morning, they sat in the kitchen together drinking tea.

"It's going to be another scorcher," Mrs. Painter said with a sigh.

"If Jessie hasn't got any water, she'll die, won't she?" he asked, his voice thick with unshed tears.

"Not yet," his mother said.

"What are we going to do?" Matt asked next.

"The police will find her," his mother replied, though she didn't sound convinced.

"I'm glad Anne's coming here. It will be another brain," Matt said. "We need all the brains we can get if we're going to find Jessie."

They went to bed again and neither woke again until the telephone rang at 9:00. At first Matt thought it was just part of a bad dream, but then he was flying down the stairs and picking up the telephone to cry, "Yes, yes, Matt Painter here." But it was only his mother's partner, Candy, wanting to know whether Mrs. Painter would watch the shop.

"Say you can't, please," Matt pleaded to his mother as he handed her the phone. She had appeared in her robe. "Jessie is more important than a shop, Mom. We must find her today or it will be too late!"

Matt's mother hesitated briefly before speaking. "I'll be by, but only for a little time," Mrs. Painter told Candy. "We've got to find Jessie—yes, Jessie," she said into the telephone.

Then, going upstairs again, Matt thought, *I've lost and the shop has won. She shouldn't be going in, not even for a minute! Mom cares more for the shop than me or Jessie.* He began adding up black marks against his mother, without really knowing it.

Almost right after that there was a knock at the door and Matt found Martin outside.

"Have you heard anything of Jessie yet?" Martin asked, wide awake in shirt and shorts.

Matt shook his head. Martin, who had no tact, said, "My dad says there's no point in looking anymore. She's as good as dead, he says, because if she lived she would recognize them and give them away. It's terrible, isn't it? Either way they've got to kill her, because a dog never forgets."

"We'll go on looking. We won't give up," replied Matt after a second of horrified silence.

"What? In this heat? My dad says he'll take us swimming this afternoon. He says it will take your mind off Jessie. What do you say, Matt?"

"I don't want my mind taken off Jessie," Matt replied. "We've been loaned a car and we're going to look for her."

"What? All over England, Scotland, and Wales?"

cried Martin. "My dad says she could be anywhere by now—even Northern Ireland. There's no knowing. But he says he's pretty sure she's dead, Matt. They won't want her to live. They're robbers."

"While there's life, there's hope, and the police are looking, too," said Matt, trying to sound brave and hopeful even though his spirits seemed to be sinking into his bare feet.

"You haven't heard Radio Norwich? The robbers switched cars. They were seen a hundred miles away in a red car," continued Martin.

"Was Jessie there?" asked Matt.

"They didn't say. But the men in the car fit the description the post mistress gave, or nearly. They were wearing the right clothes, anyway, and the police are looking for them at this very moment," said Martin.

So Jessie could be in a red car by now, except that she would have refused to get into a strange car, thought Matt. *And they wouldn't have bothered with her, anyway. Martin was probably right,* Matt thought dully. And now, the police wouldn't even be looking for the Volvo. All their attention would be on the new lead, for after all, they were looking for the robbers, not for a black Labrador with a patch of white under her chin. They wanted to catch the robbers and retrieve the money. Wasn't that their first priority? Jessie wouldn't be important to them anymore.

She would be just another lost dog, and there were hundreds of those, if not thousands, thought Matt.

"I wish you hadn't told me. I wish you had kept your stupid mouth shut, Martin," shouted Matt. "Can't you see you've made everything seem worse?"

"I can't stop things from happening, can I? Don't blame me, Matt Painter!" cried Martin. His face turned red. "It wasn't me who left the car unlocked in the parking lot, was it? Someone should knock some sense into you, Matt, before it's too late."

"I don't want sense! I want Jessie!" shouted Matt. He slammed the back door shut on Martin so hard that the house seemed to tremble.

"Oh, Matt. What was that all about?" asked his mother. She was preparing breakfast. "You shouldn't have spoken to Martin like that. He's your best friend."

"Not anymore, not ever again!" shouted Matt. "I hate him. I hate everyone—the whole world—but most of all people, just people like Martin and his father. And I want Jessie back. I want her now, all right and normal. Is that too much to ask, Mom?"

"Yes and no," replied Mrs. Painter. "You can't expect life to run smoothly all the time, love. There are always ups and downs, Matt."

"Well, this is one of those downs then, isn't it?" asked Matt glumly. He helped himself to cereal.

"Life is like the weather...it changes," continued his mother.

"Not today it isn't. It's going to be another scorcher. And did you hear what Martin said? The robbers have changed cars, so they won't be in the Volvo anymore. You know what that means? It means the police won't be looking for our car now. They'll just be keeping an eye open for it, most likely. So they won't find Jessie, not until it's too late. Not until she's dead, Mom."

"If she is still in the car," replied Mrs. Painter.

44

* * * * *

Anne's grandmother drove her to the station. There had been a brief story about Jessie in the newspaper, which arrived every morning at 8:00. The headline said, BLACK LABRADOR DISAPPEARS IN CAR STOLEN BY POST OFFICE ROBBERS. The story told of the unlocked car in a shopping center parking lot, and it noted there had been a black Labrador inside. This short piece seemed to add importance to Anne's visit.

"We must find poor Jessie. Any suggestions, Gran?" asked Anne as they left Hampstead behind.

"We must keep in touch. I will call the Battersea Dogs' Home every day," Gran replied, referring to a shelter for stray dogs.

"I hope it isn't too gloomy at Matt's," Anne said next. "I hate gloom. Personally, I think Jasper gets a raw deal. It's always Jessie, Jessie all day long, and though I love Jessie, I don't think it's fair. No one really bothers with Jasper, and he's such a lovely dog."

"Life isn't fair, darling," said Gran with a sigh. "Now you will remember to give Matt's mother the perfume, won't you? I hope it's what she likes. It's so good of them to keep having you."

"You make me sound like an unwanted pet, Gran," Anne replied.

"I didn't mean it that way. I'm sure they love having you. And Kim and I will miss you dreadfully. We always do," Gran replied. "But I know you like the country."

Getting out of the car at the station, Anne said, "There's nowhere to park, Gran. I'll be all right. Just let me get my case." And she pulled her enormous case off the backseat before adding, "I'll call you. I promise. Don't worry, Gran. I won't speak to any strangers."

The station was crowded with people, and the train was late. And all the time, without thinking, Anne was looking for Jessie.

*   *   *   *   *

By morning, Jessie had almost recovered from the worst of her injuries, but she was constantly panting from a parched throat and a terrible thirst. She was now fully conscious. The blood on her head wound had dried. And though her eyes were swollen, she could see. All she wanted now was freedom, the freedom to get out of the car and find her own way home. But the car was her prison, and for how long Jessie did not know.

Instinct told her to chew her way out of the car, but intelligence told her this was impossible, and intelligence won. So she waited for Matt to find her as he had always done in the past. She waited with the patience of an animal, without fretting. She was conserving her energy for whatever lay ahead.

Later, hearing hoofbeats on the lane outside, Jessie barked, but the three women riding past were discussing their horses and they did not hear her. Or if they did hear, the sound failed to register.

So Jessie waited for Matt, and Matt waited for news, and the day wore on.

Five

MATT took Jasper for a walk while his mother minded the shop. He had refused to go with her and felt bitter because they were doing nothing about Jessie. He had started to give up hope and was imagining his life without Jessie. He told himself he might never see her again and that he must try and love Jasper as much as he did Jessie.

But Jasper was so different. He took after his father, a rough vagabond of a dog. Jasper was impulsive and without tact, like Martin. Jasper was never quiet for more than a second. You couldn't talk to him as you could to Jessie, because Jasper would simply give you a quick, comforting lick, and then seem to say, "That's all right, then. What's next on the agenda?" Matt knew Jasper couldn't help it. He was born that way, just like Martin.

And then there was Matt's mother, who seemed to care more for the shop than for Jessie. She said she needed the money, but what was money compared with Jessie suffering? Matt was kicking at the ground now, angry with everyone.

At noon his mother returned home. "Get ready. We're picking Anne up from the station. She's arriving at 12:32. Have you forgotten?" she cried, staring at Matt's small and weary face. "Did anyone call?"

"I was out with Jasper. He can't be shut up all the time. He has to be taken out sometimes," Matt retorted rudely.

"Okay. Calm down. I'll check with the police again," Matt's mother said quietly, moving toward the telephone.

But the police had no news.

* * * * *

When she arrived at the platform, Anne saw Matt and his mother waiting. Matt's face was drawn with worry, while Mrs. Painter looked tired. Matt dragged Anne's case along the platform, while his mother asked about Anne's grandmother. Anne could feel the terrible worry hanging over both of them.

"We'll find Jessie, don't worry Matt," she said. "I'll find her, I promise."

Matt looked at her without smiling and thought, *What does she know about finding Jessie? Does she think we're idiots? Does she think we haven't tried? She makes everything sound so simple.*

"I went to the apartment. It's not like you described it, but I left Gran's address and telephone number just in case Jessie does turn up there," said Anne brightly.

When they reached the farm, Anne played ball with Jasper, while Mrs. Painter and Matt prepared lunch.

It was turning into another hot day. Anne noticed

that nothing seemed to be moving. It was as if every living thing had sought shelter from the heat. *And Jessie?* wondered Anne. *Where's Jessie?*

The Labrador had once been saved from starving to death in London, and another time from drowning under ice in the pond. And now this! It seemed to be just too much for one dog to endure in a lifetime. *Why is she so unlucky?* Anne asked herself. *Why did the robbers have to steal the car when she was inside?* But it was obvious why. The windows were wide open because Jessie needed air, so even if the car had been locked, any fool could have gotten inside. With a little knowledge or a bunch of keys, a dunce could have taken the car, Anne figured. So there really was no mystery about it. Jessie was just fated with bad luck—nothing more.

People had said Anne was unlucky, too. They said she should be living with her parents—one or the other of them—but Anne was one of those people who make the best of what is given. She felt no anger. In fact, she felt privileged to be living in London with her grandmother.

"Lunch," called Matt, holding the back door open. They ate it outside on the lawn, with their plates on their knees. Jasper sat beside Anne with his tongue hanging out.

For once, Matt and Anne didn't seem to have much to say to each other. Matt didn't feel like talking. And his mother was worrying over the shop. Candy had said Mrs. Painter wasn't pulling her weight. "We are equal partners," she had told Mrs. Painter. "But sometimes it doesn't seem like it."

"It's an emergency," Mrs. Painter had replied. "If

you had an emergency I'd stand in any time."

And smiling, Candy had said, "Yes, I know you would."

But Mrs. Painter knew Candy was right. She wasn't pulling her weight. There were too many days when Mr. Painter had to be taken to the airport, or Matt had to hang around the shop, because there was no one else at home. There were holidays and occasional business lunches, and they all got in the way of the shop. Candy's husband worked from 8 a.m. to 6 p.m. and they didn't have children, so she didn't understand.

"We need a plan," said Anne. "The telephone must be our best friend, not counting the local TV news, of course."

"And the police are still looking," added Mrs. Painter. "I called them this morning and they have not given up."

"But they're looking for the *other* car now," said Matt, dismally.

"That's not what they said," insisted Mrs. Painter.

"What about contacting veterinarians and dog shelters?" asked Anne.

"I think most of them know about it. Anyway, Jessie has a tag on her collar with our address on it," replied Mrs. Painter.

"If it hasn't fallen off," said Matt. "We're only marking time, doing nothing. Where is she? That's what I want to know. Is she dead in a ditch or wandering around trying to get home? She could be anywhere! That's what makes it so much worse. If we could say she was within a 50-mile radius of somewhere, we could start looking. But she could be anywhere in Britain, couldn't she? And that's what makes it so hopeless," said Matt. He wiped hot, angry tears from his eyes.

"They changed cars, didn't they? They robbed a post office in Bedfordshire. Look, I've got it all here," said Anne, quietly taking the newspaper clipping out of the pocket of her jeans. They read the brief story in silence.

"But I wonder how far they went before they changed cars?" mused Mrs. Painter.

"Not far, because the car was recognized, wasn't it?" asked Anne. "By 2:00, when the post office reopened, the car was reported—your car. But an hour or two later they were in a red car."

"So you mean it's hidden somewhere in Bedfordshire?" cried Mrs. Painter.

"Yes, and maybe with Jessie still inside," said Anne.

"Dying of thirst!" shouted Matt. "Because if anyone had found her, they would have called us or taken her to the police."

"Unless they had no telephone or hated the police," said Anne.

"Which isn't very likely," replied Matt.

They took their plates to the sink.

"I'll have to leave you two to man the telephone," said Mrs. Painter. "I've got to be back in the shop by 2:00. If there's any news, call me, okay?"

Matt glared. Anne said, "Yes, we'll be all right, don't worry," which made Mrs. Painter give her a hug and say, "We love having you, Anne. It makes such a difference."

"I'm going to brush Jasper and I think Elijah needs

some attention," replied Anne, looking embarrassed.

"Leave the back door open, or you won't hear the telephone," suggested Mrs. Painter on her way out.

"You mustn't give up hope, Matt," Anne said. "And your mother can't help having to go to the shop."

While they were cleaning out the barn, Janet Hinkley, a neighbor, appeared. "I'm so sorry about Jessie," she said. "I read it in the paper. You must be devastated. But I'm sure she's all right, because she's a survivor, isn't she?"

And Matt said yes, that Jessie was a survivor. Anne added that they were still looking and would probably go out in the car when it was cooler to search for her, which was news to Matt.

Then the telephone rang, and Matt rushed indoors. It was his Uncle Eric. "Lorraine and I are coming down to look for Jessie," he said.

Lorraine was Uncle Eric's wife, whom he had married after she had nursed him back to health in the hospital. Uncle Eric had been in the hospital a long time, recovering from serious injuries he received in a car crash. If not for Jessie attracting help to the accident scene, Uncle Eric might have died.

"We read about the robbery in this morning's paper and felt we must help," continued Uncle Eric. "It is your Jessie, isn't it?"

"Yes, and it's awful, really awful," Matt answered. He imagined Uncle Eric arriving, his sharp eyes flying from here to there behind his glasses. He was an inventor who, since his accident, walked with two canes. He loved Jessie, too.

"It will be great having you here, really great. When will you arrive?" asked Matt.

"Late this evening. Can you put us up?"

"Yes, of course we can," Matt replied. Matt was glad that his father was away. His father did not get along well with Uncle Eric. But now, because Uncle Eric was coming, things seemed a little better and Matt ran outside, calling to Anne, "Guess what? Uncle Eric's coming to look for Jessie, too!"

"What, the inventor? That's great!" called Anne.

The next time the telephone rang it was someone from the TV news station, wanting to interview Matt and his parents. "Yes, of course, it's all right if it will help to find Jessie," said Anne.

And so, though it was now more than 24 hours since they had lost Jessie, Matt began to feel more hopeful. "Uncle Eric will know where to look, I know he will," he said.

"And TV news goes into thousands of homes, so you must make an appeal, Matt," Anne told him. "You know, something like 'Please bring Jessie back. Please telephone us at once, please, please...'"

"You don't have to tell me what to say," replied Matt. "I know what I'm going to say. It's here in my heart."

And soon after that, before Uncle Eric and his wife Lorraine came, and before Mrs. Painter returned from the shop, a TV crew arrived. There were three in the crew and they filmed Matt holding Jasper with Elijah nearby and the farm buildings in the background. They asked Matt about Jessie and he told them how special she was. He also told them that this was the third time something awful had happened to her. His voice kept breaking with emotion. Members of the TV crew said that Willow Tree Farm was a lovely place to live and that Jessie would turn up—everyone just knew that. Anne brought the three of them iced drinks, and all the while time was passing and Jessie was still lost.

"You will put it on tonight, won't you?" Matt asked before they left. He thought he might one day like to do the job they were doing.

The one who had interviewed Matt looked at his watch and said, "We've got to edit it first, but we will do our best."

It was 3:30 now, but it seemed much later, even though the sun was still like a furnace in the sky and dusk hours away. It was too hot to take Jasper for a walk, too hot for anything but sitting in the shade and talking. Matt kept thinking of Jessie shut away somewhere, panting with thirst. At one point, he even thought that maybe it would be better if she were dead, because she wouldn't be suffering. She would be at peace, whatever that meant. But if she was dead he would like her to be buried in the garden with a gravestone and a cross, with the word "JESSIE" carved on it. He wondered if that was too much to ask. Jasper lay in the shade panting while an airplane droned overhead.

Anne was talking about a swimming pool now. "Wouldn't it be lovely to dip into one on a day like today?" she asked.

Then Mrs. Painter returned, hot and flustered. "I'm sorry I was so long," she said. "I couldn't get away. There was this woman..."

Matt didn't listen. He let Anne do the talking.

Mrs. Painter was even more bothered when she heard of Uncle Eric and Aunt Lorraine's arrival, which would be nearly any time. "Where are we going to put them?" she wailed.

But Anne said she would sleep on the sofa in the sitting room downstairs. "I don't mind a bit. I'll be nearer to things," she said. "All I need is a sleeping bag, honestly."

"Well, if you don't mind..."

"Of course I don't mind. I like being near the kitchen. I can creep in and get myself a cookie in the middle of the night," replied Anne, laughing.

Matt thought that Anne and his mother got on well together, that he might as well not be there. Then they disappeared upstairs to find a sleeping bag and Matt went outside and stood looking down the road. He hoped he might see Jessie running toward him, but of course he didn't.

The day was growing cooler at last. The flowers had stopped wilting in the heat, and in the distance cows were coming out of milking sheds and men were returning home from work. It seemed to Matt that this was the moment when things should go better. All the animals were emerging from the shade to feed again, and when he stood, tears ran down his cheeks as slowly as dew falls at evening time. He wasn't only crying for Jessie. He was also crying because his father was away, and his mother always at the shop, and now Anne had somehow shut him out and was with his mother, and always before when this had happened, he had had Jessie. He was crying, too, because Martin was no longer a friend, and because he was exhausted from lack of sleep. He let the tears come. He was alone at the roadside and no one could see him and say, "You're not crying again, Matt, are you?" as though it were a sin to cry.

Then he saw a battered car coming down the road and Uncle Eric waving out a window and shouting, "Hi Matt! Hi! How are you?"

And that's what Matt loved about Uncle Eric. He might be a bit crazy, but he was always full of gusto, whatever happened. Aunt Lorraine was driving and stopped the car to introduce herself.

"Hi there. You must be Matt," she said. "Are you well? It's nice to meet you after all this time." Uncle Eric, whose red hair was now flecked with gray, followed up with proper introductions.

Lorraine was probably older than Uncle Eric, Matt decided. She had a broad, good-natured face and the brownest eyes Matt had ever seen.

"I'm all right, thank you," Matt said to Lorraine. "It's Jessie who's in trouble."

"What about her son, Jasper? Is he all right?" asked Uncle Eric.

"Yes, he's fine," said Matt. He's just himself. Nothing really upsets Jasper."

Uncle Eric and Aunt Lorraine had never been to Willow Tree Farm before and were impressed.

"Your trees are beautiful. Look at the chestnut over there. It's wonderful," said Aunt Lorraine. And Matt, who had never really noticed the chestnut before, found himself agreeing. "It's all so old and charming," continued Aunt Lorraine. "I never thought it would be so old. Just look at the barn! Why, it's got windows, which means it was once a house upstairs. People lived there once, Matt. Just think of that."

Then Anne came bounding from the house to greet Uncle Eric. She cried, "Hello! I've always wanted to meet a real live inventor!"

And Matt's mother called, "Come in. You must be boiling. What would you like to drink?"

And Matt thought, *if only Jessie were here, I could be so happy.*

Later, they watched Matt, Jasper, and Elijah on television. The interview had been cut to half a minute. Even so, Uncle Eric said that Matt's message came over loud and clear: "Please find Jessie."

Matt didn't like the sound of his voice and kept saying, "It's awful and I look so young. Do I really look like that?"

"You look wonderful, love," said his mother. She gave him a hug.

And the others said that the interview was fine, just right, and that Jasper and Elijah looked fantastic. "Like something out of a fairy tale," said Aunt Lorraine.

But none of it brought back Jessie. There were no urgent telephone calls afterward to give them hope, nothing but the approaching end of another day without any news at all. Matt thought that nothing could make up for that—not being on television, nor having Uncle Eric and Aunt Lorraine at Willow Tree Farm. Until Jessie was found—alive or dead—a shadow would hang over everything.

Later, Uncle Eric sat on Matt's bed and talked to him, telling him that though Jessie was wonderful, she wasn't everything. He told Matt that there was always sadness in life as well as joy, and that you had to take what was handed to you like a man, "or a woman, come to think of it," he added. He told Matt that he must have a sense of proportion, and that if he scowled all the time and was miserable he would become ugly. Matt listened to him with respect, but really, he had heard it before one way or another.

* * * * *

Far away, Jessie was becoming more and more dehydrated. She could manage without food for days, but not without water. She whined and pawed at the car doors. She licked the windshield, but no moisture penetrated the locked garage and everything was silent. No footsteps stirred the gravel outside. No cars drove past. There was only the sound of busy birds and insects. And so, after a time, Jessie rested her head on her paws again and waited, wanting only one thing—to go home.

Six

A T 8:00 that evening, the telephone rang. Matt answered.

"Were you the boy who was on television tonight?" asked a voice with a thick accent.

"Yes, it was me," said Matt. Hope rose to new heights within him.

"Well, we think we've seen Jessie, down in the long meadow, just five minutes ago," the voice continued. "I rushed in to tell you right away. She's in the long meadow."

"But where is the long meadow?" cried Matt. All other conversation in the sitting room ceased. Matt repeated the name and address of a farm while an excited Anne wrote it down. Uncle Eric limped out to his car for a map.

"We'll hang on to her if we can get near enough," the voice said.

"We'll be right there!" shouted Matt, putting down the receiver.

"Okay," said Uncle Eric after studying his map. "The location is near Stowmarket. Shall we take my car to go there?"

"I'll stay behind. We can't all fit in and someone ought to man the telephone," suggested Matt's mother.

Matt found Jasper's leash, knowing Jessie's had been lost with the car. "We had better take some water, too," he said.

"She will have been drinking out of ponds. I wouldn't worry," said Uncle Eric. He picked up the map and his two canes.

Mrs. Painter handed Matt a flashlight and some change. "Call if you get delayed and please, be careful," she said, smiling at him.

"I knew television would do the trick!" shouted Anne as she got into the car.

"I can't wait for the nightmare to be over," cried Matt.

"Let's hope the man who called has really found Jessie," replied Lorraine. She turned the car and headed out.

She's distinctive—special," cried Matt. "It's got to be her!"

"We must hope, anyway," said Uncle Eric. "Let's sing," he suggested. "What shall we sing? She'll be coming 'round the mountain when she comes?"

"Yes, but it'll be Jessie coming 'round the mountain," said Anne, laughing.

"Of course," said Uncle Eric. "We mustn't forget Jessie."

So they sang, and as they did, their spirits rose.

The farm consisted of a new bungalow and several huge buildings. "But there aren't any animals," complained Anne, getting out of the car.

"They're inside those big buildings," said Matt. "But it's summer."

"They are always inside," replied Matt.

"It's called 'factory farming,'" said Uncle Eric. "The animals are kept in pens inside the buildings." He struggled to get out of the car. "And I hate it," he added.

The voice from the other end of the telephone turned out to belong to a small, broad-shouldered man of about fifty-five. He had small eyes and gray hair.

"I'll take you to the long meadow, but I don't know whether she's still there," he said.

They climbed over a gate and hurried down a rough track. Almost immediately, Matt started to call, "Jessie, Jessie," and to whistle.

"It was a little time ago," said the farmer.

Because he was disabled, Uncle Eric was waiting by the car. He imagined a world where all animals lived in green fields instead of spending their short lives in small pens, sometimes so small that they couldn't turn around.

The long meadow had been cut for hay, so they could see all the way across it, but there was no sign of Jessie. Matt stood and called. Anne said, "She's probably halfway home by now."

"Was she wearing a collar?" asked Anne.

"Yes, as far as we could see," the farmer answered in his thick accent.

"But you couldn't get near her?" asked Anne.

"No, but I kept calling to her, softly like," the farmer said.

There were no woods in the distance, just acres

and acres of land as far as the eye could see.

"Me missus said I should ring you," continued the farmer doubtfully.

"It was most kind of you," said Aunt Lorraine, hating the openness and the fields, which seemed to go on forever. She remembered the farms of her childhood, with hens scratching in yards and cows grazing in meadows.

"If I see her, I'll call you again," the farmer said. And just then, a black dog came into view, its nose to the ground in search of rabbits. Matt started to shout, "Jessie! Come here, Jessie! Jess, Jess, Jessie!" Then he ran across the long meadow, calling louder and louder, "Jessie, come here, Jessie!"

"She'll run away from you. Don't go so fast," shouted the farmer.

"No, she won't," shouted Matt. Then he was squatting and calling, and the dog turned and came toward him, and with a great lurch of disappointment he saw it wasn't Jessie. The dog was too big, and coarser, and the wrong sex.

"It isn't Jessie," he cried, biting back tears. "It's a male, not a female."

Matt took hold of the dog's collar while Aunt Lorraine began to thank the farmer. "We can't thank you enough," she said. "We've all been so worried. Jessie is like one of the family."

"Didn't you hear? It isn't Jessie," said Anne, looking at Matt's sad face. "It's a male, not a female."

"It hasn't got a tag on its collar," Matt said, dragging the dog toward them.

"But it *is* a Labrador," replied Aunt Lorraine.

"Yes, but not the right one," replied Matt.

"I'll lock it up and call the police then," said the farmer.

"You won't shoot it, will you?" Anne asked fearfully.

"Of course not. I'm not a monster," the farmer said.

"Wrong dog, then?" called Uncle Eric as they returned to the car.

"Yes, that's right," said Anne.

Matt had his head down. He couldn't bear to look at anyone now, because if he did they might see the tears of disappointment in his eyes.

"Don't worry, she'll turn up, Matt," Uncle Eric said.

They didn't sing on the way back. Matt had stopped hoping for Jessie's return. *I can't bear another disappointment,* he thought.

Anne, a survivor, kept a conversation going. She asked Uncle Eric about his inventions, and Aunt Lorraine what it was like being a nurse. Anne would never give up and nothing would ever change her.

Matt stared out the window. Another night was upon them and already he was imagining himself lying in bed thinking of Jessie. She was his best friend and could never be replaced. She never complained, nor criticized him. And however late you were, she was always pleased to see you. Matt liked Elijah, but like most goats Elijah was wildly independent, and these days his mind was mainly on food. Jasper was much the same.

But Jessie was the kindest and most faithful animal Matt had ever known—and *would* ever know— he was certain of that. Matt loved her more than Anne, and more than Uncle Eric and this new aunt he had only just met. He loved Jessie as much as his parents, or almost. And so he couldn't bear to talk as though everything was normal. He could only sit and stare out of the window while Uncle Eric's car sputtered along. They were constantly passed by newer and faster cars whose drivers rudely honked at poor Aunt Lorraine, who had only recently passed her driving test. "Why, oh why, are they so rude?" she wailed.

"Don't worry, darling," said Uncle Eric. "They're going too fast. They all go too fast. You're all right," he said. "Let them wait. It'll do them good, silly fools."

Anne chuckled at that before turning to Matt to say, "Your mom may have news. Someone may have telephoned. You must *never* give up hope. The robbers may have decided to keep Jessie. It may take time to find her, Matt. You can't be miserable all the time. She may be all right, just homesick. We'll find her, Matt, won't we, Uncle Eric?"

Uncle Eric nodded.

"Let's sing again," Anne said, "to keep up our spirits."

So they sang without Matt, mostly old songs and once, a hymn. Matt shut himself away in a blanket of misery. He was mourning already. He wanted to cry.

*   *   *   *   *

Meanwhile, Mr. Painter was already on his way home from Holland. He had made all sorts of plans in his head. First, he would console Matt. Then, he would contact the chief of police. Next, he would call the insurance company and the Automobile Association, and all the animal shelters. And if Jessie didn't show up in a couple of days he would buy Matt a new Jessie, a purebred dog, this time without a speck of white anywhere. He was willing to pay for it. He was willing to pay anything to make Matt happy again.

From the airport, Mr. Painter had called home before he left Holland so that Matt's mother would pick him up when his plane landed. He was disappointed that his call missed Matt and the others, but knew he would see them in just a few short hours. Mr. Painter couldn't wait to get home. He knew he could sort things out.

The airplane was full of other businessmen. It was a Friday and they were all looking forward to a peaceful weekend at home in the sun. Mr. Painter had to return to Holland on Monday. So he had just two days to get everything settled at home.

*   *   *   *   *

Before she left, Mrs. Painter wrote a note that read: "Gone to fetch Dad from the airport. Don't wait up." She knew that Maurice Painter would not like her brother Eric and his wife being there. Eric and Mr. Painter were very different people. Maurice Painter hated things done improperly, and Eric was the type whose suitcase was always without its handle, and whose shoes had knotted laces. So Mrs. Painter was already on edge as she set out for the airport.

At the same time, in London, an elderly couple were about to set out for a weekend in their country cottage. They were Guy and Jilly Charrington. Mr. Charrington was tall, with a military bearing and a clipped, white moustache. Mrs. Charrington was gray-haired and always wore the same string of pearls around her neck. They had a small King Charles' spaniel called Fi Fi. They piled all sorts of things into their car—tins of food, bags of groceries, plants in pots...even Fi Fi's quilted bed. They also carried a thermos with hot coffee in it and a casserole ready to pop in the oven. Once everything was loaded, they locked their small London apartment and Mrs. Charrington gave a great sigh of relief.

"Just think, in three weeks when you officially retire, we'll never have to do this again," she said. "I can't wait to live in our cottage permanently, can you, Guy?" she asked.

And Guy Charrington gave a nod before getting into the car.

Mrs. Charrington climbed into the passenger seat and kicked off her shoes. "Let's hope we've missed the rush hour and there isn't any construction on the highway," she said.

It was past dinner time, and most of the commuters and weekend travelers had already left London. *We've timed it just right,* thought Mrs. Charrington happily. In two hours we'll be there.

Mr. Charrington started to think of all the things they might have left behind. Mrs. Charrington loosened the belt on her summer dress and went to sleep.

*　　*　　*　　*　　*

In the car in the garage, Jessie whined in her sleep.

She felt weak from hunger and thirst. Her mouth and throat were parched. All the same, every few hours she sat up and barked—not once, but over and over again. Once, some boys heard her and stopped to shout through the garage doors, "Stop your yapping! There's no one here. You'll have to wait." They ran on, laughing along the horse trail.

Jessie could sense that evening was outside already. This was the time when Matt would prepare her meal, finding tempting morsels to add to it. Now and then he'd give her bits of the Sunday roast, snipped off when no one was looking, or leftovers— anything he thought she would enjoy. She would wait, watching him with her mouth watering.

"There you are. The best I can do, Jessie," Matt would whisper as he put the treat down for her in her own special dish. And then he would feed Jasper, whose dinner was likely to be large rather than tasty. That was because Jasper ate everything he was given in the same way. Even a piece of chocolate would disappear down his throat in one quick gulp, without any special appreciation. But there was no meal for Jessie tonight. She grew tired of barking and lay down with her head on her paws. She no longer bothered to listen for Matt. She hadn't given up hope. She would never do that. There just didn't seem to be any point in listening anymore.

*　*　*　*　*

Matt picked up his mother's note. "Dad's on his way here!" he shouted. "We thought he wouldn't be back till tomorrow, but Mom's picking him up now," he cried.

"Oh dear, shall we move to a hotel or something? Will we be in the way?" asked Aunt Lorraine.

"Of course not, don't be silly," said Matt. He went to the scratch pad near the telephone and looked for messages that weren't there. Anne had put the kettle on the stove.

"We had better get a late supper ready, hadn't we?" she asked.

"We'll do it, just tell us where everything is," said Aunt Lorraine. "Matt, why don't you take Jasper out? He's howling in the barn."

"He hasn't had his dinner yet, unless Mom gave it to him," said Matt.

Presently, Matt and Anne took Jasper for a walk. The whole time, and without saying anything, they were both looking for Jessie. They stared across the landscape, hoping to see a small, black Labrador returning home.

Everything seemed quiet now. The tractors were still and would be until the morning. The animals were shut away in the barns, fed and watered until the next day.

Jasper ran ahead of them, his tail curled over his back and his amber eyes staring in every direction when his nose wasn't down smelling for something. But without Jessie, Matt thought that everything seemed pointless. Jasper was all right, but he wasn't Jessie.

Anne kept stopping to look at flowers growing where once there had been hedges. The ground was hard, dry, and brittle.

Looking at Matt's dismal face, Anne said,

"Tomorrow we'll find Jessie. I feel it in my bones."

"And if we don't?" asked Matt.

"We'll go on looking. If your father's returning, we can split up into two groups. Anyway, he's sure to have a different approach. He always has. He's used to getting his own way. He won't be beaten, will he?" asked Anne.

"I don't know. I just wonder how he'll feel when he gets home. He doesn't like Uncle Eric and he's never met Aunt Lorraine," replied Matt, nervously.

But when Maurice Painter arrived he was both optimistic and friendly. He shook Uncle Eric's hand and smiled at Aunt Lorraine. Then he put an arm around Matt and said, "We'll find Jessie, and if we don't, we'll get you another Jessie, an even better one." Then he kissed Anne on the cheek.

"I don't want another Jessie. There is no such thing," Matt said. "If I can't have Jessie, I don't want another dog—not as long as I live."

"Oh, Matt, that's childish," said Mrs. Painter. "We can't always have what we want, not all the time, darling."

As though Jessie was a sort of toy, a game, a train engine, as though they were talking about a fad instead of a real live animal, Matt thought scornfully.

"We mustn't be pessimistic. We'll find her. I know we will," said Uncle Eric. He smiled at Matt.

"And Matt's absolutely right. There just couldn't be another Jessie," said Anne, with a sigh.

Then Mr. Painter went into his study to talk to the chief of police while Mrs. Painter said, "Thank God he's back. Now I'll be able to spend tomorrow in the shop. Candy is seething."

"And not help look?" asked Matt.

"For goodness sake, Matt," said Uncle Eric. "There are five of us already and two cars. We don't need your poor mother as well."

The chief of police wasn't helpful. He told Mr. Painter that he had two murders to solve and a host of burglaries, and simply could not put any more men on to find a dog. The main Automobile Association office was closed.

"We'll get up early tomorrow," said Mr. Painter, sitting down to eat, despite the late hour. "Let's get the maps out after dinner."

Then their neighbor, Janet Hinkley, called to say that she had seen Matt on TV and wondered if there was anything she could do to help. Matt answered and said, "Just keep an eye open for Jessie, please, all the time. We are all looking. We won't stop till we find her, dead or alive, not ever..."

But even as he said it, Matt knew it wasn't true. His father already was set to buy him a new Jessie, another Labrador to love. His father didn't understand that every time Matt looked at a Labrador from now on he would be reminded of only one thing—the real Jessie.

Seven

MRS. Charrington put her shoes back on as her husband steered the car toward the garage at their weekend cottage. "Everything smells so lovely here, so fresh," she exclaimed, getting out of the car to open the garage doors.

Mr. Charrington flexed his neck. He felt stiff all over. *I'm getting old,* he thought, *and I don't like it.*

Birds were singing by the cottage, and the high hedges were green and beautiful. A great oak spread a circle of shade on the small lawn beyond the cottage.

"I wish you had retired already, Guy," Mrs. Charrington said to her husband. She pulled at the garage doors, then stopped and stared. "Guy, Guy!" Mrs. Charrington called. "Come and look! There's a car here, a strange car. Look, Guy, hurry!"

"There can't be," said Mr. Charrington, getting out of the car slowly. "You're imagining things. How can there be a car in our garage? Don't be ridiculous."

"But there is," shouted Mrs. Charrington. "And there's a poor dog inside, a poor old Labrador. Hurry, Guy!" While she waited for her husband, she mur-

mured to Jessie, "Poor dog, poor old doggie, what are you doing here?"

"My goodness, you're right," said Mr. Charrington, coming up behind his wife. "A strange car in our garage. But how did it get here? And the dog!"

"That's what I told you, but you never listen," Mrs. Charrington retorted. "We had better get the dog out. It's got blood on its head. Look—the whole backseat is covered with blood."

Mrs. Charrington opened the Volvo's door inch by inch, talking all the time. Fi Fi began barking hysterically in the other car.

"It's all right, doggie. I'm your friend," said Mrs. Charrington in a comforting tone.

Jessie moved slowly toward her, for at that moment all she wanted was water. Nothing else mattered.

"It seems impossible, a car and a dog in our garage!" said Mr. Charrington. "I'd better call the police. What do you think, shall I call the police?"

"I don't care," said his wife. "I only care about this poor dog. Get Fi Fi's leash, Guy, and hurry!" she cried.

A moment later Jessie was out of the car, a poor battered Jessie, her neck and head covered with dried blood and her walk unsteady.

"Gently does it, let's get her into the cottage," said Mrs. Charrington. "Have you got the back door key, Guy?"

Mr. Charrington, his mind still numbed by hours of driving, unlocked the back door and took a look inside. "Everything's normal," he said. "We haven't been robbed, so why the car in the garage?"

"With a dog inside, and it's the dog that matters!"

cried Mrs. Charrington. She urged Jessie inside, then
shut the back door.

"Now first of all, she needs water. She's parched.
All that blood lost and nothing to eat or drink—it's
criminal. I would like to report her owners!" Mrs.
Charrington cried while filling a dish with water.

"Just look at her," Mrs. Charrington continued.
"She's dying of thirst. How could anyone do such a
thing? And look at her head. It's all out of shape."

"Perhaps there was a car crash," suggested Mr.
Charrington.

"What, in our garage, Guy? Don't be ridiculous,"
said Mrs. Charrington.

She turned her attention to Jessie. "A little bread
and milk might help this poor dog, I think. Have you
brought the boxes in from the car yet, Guy?" de-
manded Mrs. Charrington.

Jessie looked around the kitchen uneasily. She was
afraid this was going to be a new home, and she didn't
want a new home. She wanted to be back at home,
which she loved. She wanted her own bed. She
wanted Matt and Jasper, and she wanted Will bring-
ing her treats in the morning. But she ate the bread
and milk in three quick gulps. Then she licked Mrs.
Charrington's small, plump hands, which was Jessie's
way of saying, "Thank you."

Mrs. Charrington slowly eased the collar off of
Jessie. "There's an address. Look, Guy," she called.
"Let's try and track down the phone number that
goes with the address, and then call the police."

* * * * *

Matt crawled into bed and thought, *another day*

gone and still no Jessie. He imagined his father buying a new Labrador. He imagined a small puppy looking at him, a champion he could show, one who would produce valuable puppies. It would be the sort of dog his father called "an investment"—a real pedigree puppy, not a reject picked half-drowned out of a stream like Jessie.

Matt knew his father was trying to be kind. He had been quite different lately—much, much nicer. Mom had said that it was because he had an easier job now. "It's rewarding, too," she had said. But Mr. Painter still didn't seem to understand that Matt couldn't be consoled so easily.

He thinks I'm shallow, and in a way that's an insult, Matt thought now, lying in bed. *And supposing Jessie turns up, after all? What will she think if a new Labrador is in her place, using her bed, her brush and comb, and water bowl? Won't it break her heart?*

And yet on Sunday, Matt's father was going to take them all to some kennels just 50 miles away to find a new Jessie. He thought he was being kind and generous, and pointed out that if Jessie wasn't back by Sunday it was almost certainly because she was dead.

Anne was downstairs in the sitting room, getting her bed prepared for the evening. The garden outside was full of night sounds. Rabbits were scratching about in one of the flower beds and bats kept flying past the windows. In the distance, an owl hooted.

Before getting into bed Anne knelt to pray: "Please God, find Jessie. Please God, bring her back safe

74

before Sunday. And please God, make sure Gran is all right."

Anne was very tired. Uncle Eric was the most tiring person she had ever met, because he never stopped talking. And then there was the tension hanging over Willow Tree Farm. Matt was trying to stifle his feelings, trying not to shout at his father, "I don't want another Jessie! Can't you understand?" Matt's mother, meanwhile, worried about the shop, torn between it and Matt. And Matt's father was frantically trying to get everything cleared up and everyone happy before he returned to Holland on Monday morning. Then there was Uncle Eric, sadly hobbling about with his two canes while his wife Lorraine tried to fit in.

I wish I were back in London, thought Anne. She sighed and snuggled under her cover. *There's no peace here, and there won't be until Jessie returns— if she ever does.*

Meanwhile, Mrs. Painter was trying to tell her husband that Matt wasn't ready to replace Jessie. "He must have time to get over losing Jessie, Maurice," she said.

"But I want to stop him from mourning," replied Mr. Painter. "You have enough on your mind without an unhappy son. Can't you see I want you to be happy? Both of you. A friend of mine just lost a son and it's made me realize how much you and Matt mean to me. Without you both, I would be lost. I know that," said Mr. Painter, looking out between the curtains. He could see rabbits on the lawn. "I love this place. I just wish I could be here all the time," he added.

He was just climbing into bed when the telephone rang. Anne called from downstairs, "I'll answer it, it's probably Gran." Gran often stayed up till one in the morning to write letters, insisting that she was not old enough for an early bedtime.

"Willow Tree Farm here," said Anne, picking up the receiver.

"This is Guy Charrington speaking," said the voice on the other end. "I think we've got your dog. Have you lost a Labrador? She's in pretty poor shape, I'm afraid. She's got a nasty wound on her head."

"But she's still alive?" asked Anne excitedly. Suddenly, the whole household seemed to be gathering around her as she stood barefoot in her pajamas. She held her hand over the mouthpiece of the telephone and quickly told the others what Mr. Charrington had just described.

"Your address was on her collar tag and my wife's bathing her wounds now. You don't know who the car belongs to, do you?" asked Mr. Charrington. "I'm just about to call the police."

"It's ours," Anne said without thinking. "But you had better call the police anyway because they're looking for it."

Then Mr. Painter seized the receiver. "This is Mr. Painter here. Where are you exactly?"

But instead of giving directions, Mr. Charrington said, "She can stay here till morning. Don't come out now. We had to call directory assistance to locate your telephone number, and we're tired out. My wife says she'll look after the dog. The animal's not fit to travel anyway."

Mr. Charrington took a breath and continued,

"She's a pitiful sight—she had no food, no water, and there was blood all over the car. I don't know how she got here, but someone should be prosecuted."

"We must get her now!" shouted Matt. He pulled on his father's arm. "We can't wait till morning, please!"

"She's not fit to travel," whispered Anne.

"I'll wrap her up. I'll carry her to the car," pleaded Matt.

"Well, if you're sure you don't mind keeping her," Mr. Painter said into the telephone. Matt stood beside his father, whispering in his free ear, "We must get her now, *please*, Dad."

"We're awfully tired," said Mr. Charrington. "We're not youngsters anymore, and we are a long way from you. If you were to leave right now, you wouldn't be here till past midnight, if not 1:00. We've just come down from London. We both need sleep. Do you mind leaving it till morning?"

"No, of course not," Matt's father answered. "I'll just get a pencil and paper and write down your address," he said.

"Jessie'll be all right, Matt," said Uncle Eric, patting the boy's shoulder. "The people who found her sound kind."

"Yes, but she's hurt," Matt said.

Mr. Painter was writing on a piece of paper now. "Yes, you *are* a long way from here, at least 80 miles. We'll make an early start, then. When do you get up?" he asked Mr. Charrington.

"Eight o'clock—not a minute before eight, if you don't mind," said Mr. Charrington. "We're getting on, you know. My wife has given your dog bread and milk,

77

and we'll give her one of Fi Fi's tins of dog food before we go to bed. She's a lot better than she was. She'll be all right by morning. What do you call her, by the way?"

"Jessie," said Mr. Painter.

When he had put down the receiver, Mr. Painter and the others went into the kitchen and drank mugs of tea and wondered about Jessie.

"I was so worried about her that I forgot to ask about the car," said Mr. Painter.

"Somebody must have hit her hard if there was blood in the car," said Matt slowly. And as he drank the tea, he knew he would not sleep all night.

They were all wide awake now. They sat in the kitchen and talked. Anne told them about her grandmother's dog, Kim. Eric told them about a new invention he had in mind. "It will revolutionize bicycling. It's tiny, so tiny that you can carry spare batteries in your pocket. It will take the hard work out of rides. It will cut traveling time dramatically," he said.

Mrs. Painter told them about the shop, about Candy's temper tantrums, and about awkward customers. Mr. Painter told them about his job, and Aunt Lorraine told them how difficult it was working in a hospital, where there was never enough time to do everything you felt you should do. And Matt told them about school, about a new teacher who couldn't keep order.

They drank mug after mug of tea, celebrating.

It was nearly 2:00 when at last Matt went to bed.

In a few hours we'll have Jessie back, thought Matt as he plumped his pillow. *Then life will be normal again. That's all I want.*

* * * * *

The next thing he knew, his mother was shaking him and crying, "Wake up, Matt! We've overslept. All of us. Half the morning's gone. None of us woke up, none of us. It's awful."

"But what about Jessie?" shouted Matt.

"And the shop," said his mother. "Candy called me—that's what woke us up. After you went to bed we sat up and talked some more. Oh, do hurry, Matt!" cried his mother.

Sunlight filtered through the curtains. Matt sprang out of bed, his heart thudding, his eyes still heavy with sleep. Swiftly, he drew back the curtains. The day was well under way, and the chickens were scratching on the lawn. Will had let out Jasper and tied up Elijah, and was now working in the yard.

Pulling on clothes, Matt rushed downstairs, crying, "Can we go now, right away?"

His father was at the kitchen sink. "Don't get nervous," he said to Matt. "I'll call the Charringtons. Jessie will be all right."

Uncle Eric was devouring cereal as though he hadn't eaten for days. Matt's mother was picking up her car keys.

"You can't take the car, Mom!" Matt shouted. "We need it to get Jessie."

"We'll take you to the shop in our car, Sis," said Uncle Eric. Just hang on a minute."

Matt didn't want to eat. He only wanted one thing—Jessie. Through the window he could see Anne playing with Jasper on the lawn.

Mr. Painter was calling the Charringtons to apologize. Mrs. Charrington answered, "That's all right, dear. We'll be here. She won't run away. Don't worry," she said.

"There you are, no hassle," Mr. Painter told Matt. He smoothed down his son's hair.

Anne came in with Jasper. "We can take him with us, can't we? I'll look after him," she said. "And don't look so worried, Matt. Everything's going to be all right from now on."

"Yes, you can bring Jasper," said Mr. Painter. He turned toward Matt. "Just the three of us will go. Your mother's got to be at the shop and Uncle Eric and Aunt Lorraine are going to have a lazy day in the garden."

Uncle Eric was searching for his car keys now, turning the place upside down. "You lose everything," complained Aunt Lorraine. "I told you to give them to me."

Matt's father started frying bacon and eggs, while Anne poured everyone coffee. Jasper lay in the way, panting.

"There won't be time for lunch later, so have something to eat now, Matt," said his mother. She saw that Uncle Eric had found his keys, and followed him out the door, combing her hair as she went.

"Why did we oversleep? Why?" cried Matt.

"We stayed up late, that's why," said Anne.

"It's not the first time this has happened. It's becoming a habit. Why didn't we set clocks? Why are we so incompetent?" shouted Matt.

"Calm down," replied Anne.

Will entered the kitchen then. "I didn't wake you. I thought you needed the sleep. I've been here since 8:00," he said.

"But we needed waking. We're fetching Jessie. She's been found," cried Matt.

"Well, how could I know that?" asked Will. His voice was sullen.

It was nearly 2:00 when at last they went out to the car. Uncle Eric had long since returned from dropping Mrs. Painter off at the shop, and Matt could only think about Jessie—was she all right? Would she recover from her ordeal? And then, when finally they were all in the car, with their seat belts fastened and Jasper trying to lick Anne's face and the sun bearing down, the engine wouldn't start.

Mr. Painter jumped out and threw open the hood of the car. Matt started to shout, "I knew this would happen! I knew it! We should have gone last night. Now we'll never see Jessie. She'll have given up hope and died. I know she will. But you all had to have proper breakfasts, and do your hair, and wait for the mail and, and..."

Matt's voice trailed off. He couldn't say anything more because suddenly he felt completely limp with disappointment.

"Keep calm," said Anne. "The car will start in a minute."

Uncle Eric said, "Won't it start? Give it a kick, or take my car, Maurice. Go on, it's got a full tank of gas."

But Mr. Painter wouldn't be caught dead in Eric's old car, and besides, he was certain that the car would start any minute. He believed it only needed an adjustment here and an adjustment there. There couldn't be anything basically wrong with it, he told himself. The car was quite new.

Matt stood in the driveway, imagining Jessie waiting for him with her nose pressed against a door. He pictured her with a gaping wound on her head. He felt as though his heart was breaking.

Eight

"THIS is a useless car. Can't we get a mechanic to help, or go in Uncle Eric's, or rent a car?" cried Matt.

Time was slipping by quickly.

But before anything more happened, Mrs. Painter rejoined the group. Candy, wearing jeans and a pink shirt, had brought her back from the shop sooner than planned.

"I suddenly remembered our Volvo, stuck out there in some stranger's garage, and thought I had better go with you after all," said Mrs. Painter. "One of us will have to drive it back while the other returns in this car. And I thought you might just still be here," she said. "Anyway, it's too hot for anyone to shop now."

After looking at the stalled car, Candy said, "I can't take you because I must get back to the shop. Though no one's likely to come in, I must be there just the same."

It was growing hotter all the time, but at last the car's engine came to life. Matt rushed indoors to fetch dog biscuits for Jessie. Anne put on sun glasses before fetching Jasper, who had been shut in the barn. They piled into the car. Uncle Eric waved good-bye. Jasper climbed onto the backseat and snuggled up against Anne.

"Drive faster, Dad," Matt said.

"We're so late already another half an hour won't make any difference," said Anne.

"I feel as though we've let Jessie down. She must have been waiting and waiting," said Matt.

"Animals don't mind waiting," said Mrs. Painter. "Look at horses. They are always waiting for something—to be fed, or exercised, or just for the sun to go down. But I'm sorry about the delays, Matt. I really am. Candy's looking for another partner, but I don't mind. I'm sick of the shop. There's a job opening at the local primary school for a part-time secretary and I'm applying for it." Mrs. Painter smiled. "That way I'll be at home all through the holidays."

It was long past 4:00 and none of them had eaten since their very late breakfast. Matt shut his eyes and wished he could sleep and wake up to find Jessie beside him. Instead, there was Jasper, giving off heat like a furnace. But he was so pleased to be with them that he was trying desperately to keep still, his tongue hanging out, his eyes looking straight ahead.

Anne kept nodding off and dreaming about London. Matt fidgeted.

"Oh, for goodness sake, stop fussing. Just relax, Matt," said his mother. "You look so miserable. After all, we *have* found Jessie, and we are on our way to fetch her, even if we are a bit late. Isn't that enough? In less than an hour now the whole beastly episode

84

will be over, and I'm telling you now, I'm never taking Jessie with us ever again on a hot day, no matter what you say."

Just then, the car began to move in jerks. Another minute and Matt shouted, "It's not going to stop again, is it Dad? Oh, I simply don't believe it!"

Mr. Painter steered the car onto the shoulder of the highway, while other cars whistled by at 70 and 80 miles an hour.

"We are dogged by fate," said Mrs. Painter. "It must be in our stars, so we can't do anything about it. We're just unlucky."

But Matt wasn't prepared to accept fate. He yelled, "Get it going, *please*, Dad. How far is it to Jessie? I'm going to hitch. I'm not trusting this car a minute longer."

Matt began to push his way out of the car. Jasper, sensing trouble, began barking wildly.

"Watch how you get out of the car," shouted Mr. Painter, mindful of the traffic roaring by them. "Don't get out into the traffic or you'll be cut to pieces." Mr. Painter's face was running with sweat.

"This has never happened to us before. Why today?" wailed Mrs. Painter, though she had already said it was fate.

Matt began to try and hitch a ride. He stood at the side of the road, holding up an arm. But his mother would have none of it. She got out and pulled him back to the car.

"Give me the map, then. I'm going to walk," Matt shouted, his face scarlet with heat and frustration. "I can read a map. I don't need any of you!"

"How far is it?" Anne asked Matt. "I'll go with you,

Matt," she offered.

They fetched the map from the car. Mr. Painter had circled in red the approximate area where he thought the Charringtons' cottage was, and he had drawn a very wide circle.

"It must be at least 10 miles," he said. "You'll never make it."

"I knew we should have called a mechanic from the garage, or taken Uncle Eric's car," shouted Matt. "I said so, but no one ever listens to me."

"Come on, we can start walking," said Anne. "They can catch up to us in the car." And ignoring Matt's mother's objections, they started walking along the grassy shoulder, with Jasper straining ahead. At least the heat had dropped off some.

"I hate cars," said Matt. "They always let you down. I never want a car. I shall go everywhere on a bike when I'm grown up."

"I shall have a pony and carriage," said Anne.

"Don't accept a ride from anyone, do you hear?" shouted Matt's mother. She looked small from a distance. "Not from anyone. Are you listening, Matt?"

Matt waved at her impatiently and grumbled to Anne, "Why are they like that? Why haven't I got sensible parents?" He was striding ahead of Anne, his thoughts now centered only on Jessie.

"They're all right. You expect too much, Matt," Anne said.

Cars tore by. They were full of people on their way home from a day out. In a field, a small crowd was clearing up after a horse show.

"I wish I had grandparents," Matt muttered. "Other people have grandparents. They go and stay with their grandparents."

"Well, you know you can stay with us in London any day," Anne said.

But Matt hated London. He hated the endless roar of the traffic, the choked streets, and the rushing people. There didn't seem to be enough space in London.

"We ought to sing to keep our spirits up," suggested Anne. But Matt wouldn't sing and his legs were already aching. It now seemed like years had passed since Jessie and the Volvo had been taken by robbers.

They stopped to look at the map. The Charringtons' weekend home was called End Cottage, though it wasn't specifically shown on the map. But Anne judged its approximate location and said, "It's not far now, look."

"Yes, but that's the outside of the circle," replied Matt.

Anne pointed out, however, that the map was six miles to an inch, and because the whole circle was less than an inch, End Cottage couldn't be that much farther. She began to sing a popular rock-and-roll song, and then a song from a recent musical in London. After a while, they turned off the road down a narrow, tree-lined road. On each side, large black-and-white cows wandered in lush grass.

"I would like to live here, because there are lots of trees and hedges," Matt said.

But Anne told Matt he was being ungrateful. "Willow Tree Farm is a dream of a place," she said. "And look what you've got there, Matt—chickens, a goat, and two dogs."

"You've said that before," replied Matt.

"One needs to keep saying it to you. You just don't know how lucky you are," retorted Anne. "My grandmother's got her dog, of course. But I would love a dog of my own, and a goat, and chickens. I would have a pony as well. I would spend all my time with the animals—my animals. I haven't got anything of my own, not a single animal, not even a goldfish."

Beyond the lush field stood a stately home with splendid trees around it, and an acre of garden nicely bordered by a wall. Anne imagined horses and carriages in front of it. She imagined herself living there. Matt was very tired now. He had to run to keep up with Anne, who was older and taller. Then Anne stopped to point at the house. "That's where I would like to live," she said.

"Big deal," replied Matt, looking at the sky. "It's going to be dark soon and then we'll never find the Charringtons' cottage and Jessie. And Dad will be furious and so will Mom," he said.

"Well, we're not lost yet, not truly anyway," replied Anne. She had hardly gotten the words out of her mouth when a small truck stopped beside them and a man leaned out. He wore a cap and had two hunting dogs in the back.

"Want a lift?" he asked.

Anne shook her head. "No, thanks. We're looking for what's known as 'End Cottage,'" she said.

"I don't know it," said the man. He drove on.

"We should have given him the Charringtons' name," said Matt. "He might have known the location by their name."

"Yes, I guess we should have," replied Anne.

"I feel like we're walking in circles," said Matt. "I don't think we're getting anywhere. I think we'll still be walking tomorrow morning, that's what I think."

"We shouldn't have left the car," said Anne.

"Well, it was your idea," replied Matt.

"No, it wasn't. It was yours, so it's all your fault," said Anne.

"Liar," shouted Matt.

They glared at each other, then walked on without speaking. Two more cars passed them, then an old woman on a bicycle. She stared at them as if they had just arrived from Mars.

Curtains were being drawn now in scattered cottages. A man was taking a dog for its final walk that day. Matt thought the day had lasted forever. Anne was thinking fate was still against them.

"I want to sit down somewhere and go to sleep, and then wake up and find Jessie licking my face—that's all I want in the whole world," Matt said. He rubbed his eyes wearily.

"Do you think that beastly car is going yet?" he asked Anne. "Do you think Mom and Dad are waiting for us at End Cottage, fuming?"

"I don't think End Cottage exists," Anne replied sarcastically. "I think the Charringtons are enemies of yours who want to taunt you, that's what I think."

They didn't say anything more for a long while. They just kept walking.

* * * * *

Seven miles away, Mr. Painter continued to tinker beneath the hood of the car. Mrs. Painter had wanted to call a mechanic from a garage. But every time she was about to look for a telephone, the car's engine sputtered to life again, only to fail a minute later.

A young man in a suit had helped for a while, and a lady had offered to contact the Automobile Association for them, but Mr. Painter refused the offer. He was certain that the car was about to start any minute, and so it had seemed at the time. And all the while they both worried about Anne and Matt.

"We shouldn't have let them go," said Mrs. Painter over and over again. Mr. Painter took his anxiety out on the car, kicking it now and then and muttering under his breath.

Then suddenly, he discovered what was wrong. "It's the gas pump!" he shouted. "It's a faulty connection. The gas isn't getting through. What a dunce I've been!"

A minute later he slammed the hood shut and cried, "Okay, we're off. Jump in and look at the map."

"The children took the map, Maurice," Mrs. Painter reminded him. "So we haven't got a map now."

"But we've got an address and that's what matters. We'll find it all right," said Mr. Painter. "Not to worry. I'll get you there."

* * * * *

"Poor, old Jessie, it doesn't look like they're coming for you," said Mrs. Charrington. She felt like they'd been waiting a lifetime for the Painters to show up. "They don't care," she said. "And you're doing so poorly."

"We'll keep her if you like," said Mr. Charrington. "I've always wanted a Labrador."

"And she's no trouble. She'll be a good guard dog," replied Mrs. Charrington.

The curtains were drawn in the cottage to keep out the late afternoon sun. Jessie had been listening for Matt all day. Despite her appearance, her strength was slowly returning and the wound on her head was healing already. She wanted only to go home.

Mr. Charrington called Jessie 'old girl.' Mrs. Charrington fussed over her, continually emptying and refilling her water bowl. Horses trotted past the cottage and down the lane. The police detectives had checked out the Volvo and left a long time ago. The day was ending and there was no Matt. Jessie stood up and shook herself, then went to the back door, asking to be let out.

"She needs to get out for a bit, I expect. I'll get a leash," said Mrs. Charrington.

Once outside, Jessie smelled the air and knew that though she was far from home, she had to go soon if she was ever to see Matt again.

"She's not used to us yet," said Mrs. Charrington, dragging Jessie back indoors. "She wants to be off. I can feel it. Don't let her out, Guy, or we'll lose her, and I must take Fi Fi for a walk. He's been asking for hours, poor thing."

But Mr. Charrington wasn't listening. His wife talked so much that he rarely listened. It was just too much effort and anyway, he wasn't interested in most of what she said.

"You go, dear. I'm going to do some gardening

before it's dark," he replied. "I'll mow the lawn to-morrow."

Fi Fi ran ahead of Mrs. Charrington, yapping and jumping. Jessie lay with her head on her paws. The sun was going down in a great, red ball of fire.

Matt and Anne were less than two miles away now. They were running and walking, their eyes looking for a narrow lane with a cottage at the end, appropriately named End Cottage. But Jessie didn't know that.

"I don't know why I'm suddenly so excited. I don't know what I'm expecting," Matt said, "but I'm somehow certain that we are on the right road at last."

"So am I!" cried Anne. She looked at her watch and thought about how late it was.

A mile away, Mr. and Mrs. Painter had stopped the car and were wondering which way to go next. "You shouldn't have let them go ahead," said Mr. Painter for the fifth time.

Mrs. Painter replied, as she had before, "You could have stopped them, Maurice. You saw them go. But if something happens to them I'll never forgive myself."

*　*　*　*　*

Mr. Charrington scratched at one of the ornamental shrubs with a hoe, then went indoors to get the plant food they had brought with them from London. He wasn't really thinking of anything in particular at that moment, and wandered in and out of the cottage without bothering to close the back door after him.

Jessie sniffed the air, then padded softly through the open door, her legs still a little unsteady but her brain telling her it was time to go. She turned down the bridle path, swaying a little as she walked. Her head ached and her back was stiff with pain.

A moment later, Mr. Charrington looked around the kitchen and then called out, "Jessie? Where are you, old girl? Not gone, have you? Not gone already?" Then he rushed outside to his wife and called out, "Jilly, Jessie's gone, she's left us!"

Mrs. Charrington was very angry. She called Mr. Charrington a silly old fool, then dialed the Painters' number and waited. Eventually, Uncle Eric answered. "It's about the dog," Mrs. Charrington said. "We waited and waited and now she's got away."

"What, Jessie?" exclaimed Uncle Eric. "But aren't they there yet? They left home hours ago! Oh dear, oh dear, there must have been an accident—they left before three. Oh, goodness, what are we going to do?" he cried.

"Well, she's gone," repeated Mrs. Charrington, who seemed not to care much about what Uncle Eric was saying. "We've kept her here all day. We've fed her and bathed her head wound, and if you can't be bothered to collect her, well, that's that."

"But I've just told you..." began Uncle Eric, trying to explain once more. But Mrs. Charrington had already banged down the receiver.

Uncle Eric shouted for his wife. "There must have been an accident. They've never picked up Jessie, and now she's gone!" he cried. "Oh, what a disaster! What an awful disaster! What shall we do? What can we do? Oh, I feel so helpless with these sticks!" he shouted, hitting at the air with his canes.

"Keep calm, Eric. You'll send your blood pressure up," said Aunt Lorraine. "We can't do anything. We can only wait."

"But I *must* do something! I don't want to wait. It's feeble to do nothing. We had better call the police. They may have been in an accident."

"We can't do anything if they have," Aunt Lorraine pointed out gently. They'll be in a hospital somewhere."

* * * * *

"There it is! Look!" shouted Matt. "Look, there's a sign saying End Cottage! We've made it! We've walked all the way. Come on, let's run."

And they all ran, Jasper leading the way and barking with excitement.

Matt rushed to the back door of the Charringtons' cottage. He shouted, "Jessie, I'm here! We've arrived! Everything's going to be all right."

Then Mrs. Charrington appeared around the side of the cottage.

"We've come for Jessie," said Matt, smiling broadly. "I'm sorry we're so late."

"Late! You call this late?" cried Mrs. Charrington, sarcastically. "Is that what you call it? Well, she's gone."

"Gone?" shouted Matt. "But how, and why?"

"You had better ask yourself that," retorted Mrs. Charrington. "Personally, I don't think you're fit to have a dog."

"When did Jessie go? How long ago?" asked Anne

faintly. She watched the tears rolling down Matt's face.

"Some time ago," said Mr. Charrington, who had appeared behind his wife. "It was my fault," he continued. "You had better come in. You both look exhausted."

Anne began to cry, too, and she hardly ever cried. "We overslept, but then we tried so hard to get here, we tried and tried, but everything was against us," she sobbed. "It was as though a black cloud hung over our heads. You needn't believe us if you don't want to, but it's the truth, I'll swear to it on a Bible if you like."

Mrs. Charrington seemed unmoved. "Well, your Jessie was hit with something—probably the spade from our garage. It's a wonder the dog isn't dead," she said, leading the way into the sitting room. "Whoever did it should be put in prison for life! He isn't fit to be out among decent people. I'm surprised he didn't kill the post mistress as well. And as for you two, you should be ashamed of yourselves for taking so long to get here. This isn't a boarding kennel, you know."

"Steady on," said Mr. Charrington. "We all make mistakes, you know."

Mrs. Charrington glared at her husband. "Now look who's talking," she replied.

Matt and Anne looked at each other. They had come so far, and for this?

"Come home, Jessie," Matt whispered, not caring if anyone overheard him, not caring if he sounded foolish. "Please, just come home."

Nine

UNCLE Eric called the nearest police station, but no one there had heard of an accident.

"If you must call around, try Bedfordshire. That's where they were headed," said Aunt Lorraine. "But really, there isn't any point in calling, anyhow."

But Uncle Eric had to do something. He couldn't sit still and imagine his sister, brother-in-law, Matt, and Anne lying in a ditch, terribly injured, without doing anything about it.

The Bedfordshire police were not very helpful, either. "There was an accident on the highway at nine this morning," the duty officer said.

Uncle Eric replied crossly, "But that's too early. It would have to have been an accident that took place after 2:00."

The policeman on duty spoke soothingly. "Don't worry, sir, you'll hear soon enough if there's been an accident," he said.

"I'll try the hospitals next," said Uncle Eric, putting down the receiver.

"We can't do anything, love," said Aunt Lorraine.

"I expect that their car has just broken down."

But Uncle Eric was too wound up now to stop trying. He called directory assistance and obtained the number of seven hospitals, then called them one after another. At one, the receptionist was quite angry and shouted that Uncle Eric wasn't speaking to an accident hospital at all. "We are a maternity unit," she said.

"You never think an accident will happen until it happens to you," he said wearily. "And after that, you're afraid all the time."

"They'll be all right," said Aunt Lorraine in a soothing tone. "They're all together and Maurice is a very competent person."

"I love Jessie, you know that," said Uncle Eric. "She saved my life when I had my crash. If she hadn't barked and barked for help, I would have died in my car. They said that at the hospital, didn't they? They said that if I hadn't been found, I would have been dead in a few more hours."

Aunt Lorraine nodded. "Let's sit in the garden. We'll be back in London tomorrow and it's a shame to miss the country air."

* * * * *

"There it is, look over there!" cried Mr. Painter. "End Cottage."

"I just hope the kids are there," replied Mrs. Painter, "because if they aren't, I think I'm going to have a nervous breakdown." Her face was lined with fatigue, and her hands shook slightly from nerves.

Mr. Painter knocked on the Charringtons' door.

Matt opened it, his face wet with tears. "We're too late, she's gone," he said. He held a bun in one hand. Anne stood behind him drinking orange juice.

"You had better come in," said Mrs. Charrington. She guided Mr. and Mrs. Painter in.

"Jessie's gone?" repeated Mrs. Painter. "But how, and where?"

"Tea or coffee?" asked Mrs. Charrington, not bothering to answer Mrs. Painter.

"Tea, thank you very much," said Mrs. Painter. Her face had turned the color of putty, and she began to stumble. In another second, she slid to the floor and lay silently in a heap.

Matt screamed, while Mrs. Charrington hurriedly fetched a cushion and put it under Mrs. Painter's head. "Get a glass of water, Guy! Don't gape," Mrs. Charrington ordered.

"Everything's been too much for your mother, Matt. It's just been far too much," said Anne.

Mr. Painter, his own face like ash, knelt beside his wife.

What have we done to deserve this? thought Matt, shocked to see his mother doing so poorly. *Someone tell me, please.*

He wiped his face with his hands, while Jasper whined by the door and Fi Fi yapped constantly in another room. The cottage seemed too small for them all, and too tidy. Whenever Jasper moved, Matt worried he would bump something over.

"Sit, Jasper, sit," Anne said in a firm voice.

Mrs. Painter, embarrassed, finally sat up. "I don't know what came over me," she said. "I'm so sorry."

Matt tried to give his mother an encouraging smile,

but already his thoughts were turning back to Jessie. He couldn't taste the bun he was eating. It was dusk now. Soon, it would be dark, and Jessie was still missing. Eating buns and drinking tea was wasting time, and they had to find Jessie soon if they were to find her at all.

As if he could read Matt's mind, Mr. Painter began looking at his map again. "If we're lucky, Jessie might have taken the route through Steggals Wood. That's the shortest way," he said, pointing at the map. "If we drive around the far side of the woods we might just meet her coming out."

Mr. Charrington agreed. "There's a fence around the wood, but it's only barbed wire and she can get through it," he said.

"Come on then, Matt," said Mr. Painter.

"What about Mom?" Matt asked uncertainly.

"Can she stay here?" asked Mr. Painter, switching on the smile that charmed customers from all over the world.

"Yes, of course," said Mrs. Charrington. She was instantly enchanted.

"No problem, delighted," replied Mr. Charrington at the same moment.

"I'm going out with Jasper, on up the lane. He needs a walk," said Anne.

"It's only a bridleway," said Mrs. Charrington.

Mr. Painter looked at his watch. It was very late now. "We'll meet back here in 45 minutes, then," he said.

"You had better take a flashlight, Anne," suggested Mr. Charrington. "Hang on while I get you one."

Matt had stopped crying. For once, he wasn't really

thinking about Jessie. His mind was a blank, and he was glad because that way he wouldn't cry.

His father patted him on the shoulder. "We'll find her, son," he said. But Matt didn't believe him anymore. He didn't believe anyone. He was so tired he could hardly keep his eyes open, and his legs ached unbearably. But he followed his father to the car and sat beside him on the front seat.

If it breaks down again, we're sunk, he thought, *but somehow I don't really care anymore. I've got no fight left in me, that's what it is. I'm just too tired.*

Mr. Painter drove slowly down the country lanes. He was tired, too, but didn't show it. He had been brought up to hide his feelings.

"If we don't find her, what are we going to do?" asked Matt miserably.

"We will find her."

"I don't want another Labrador, not ever," Matt said. "You know that, Dad, don't you?"

Mr. Painter nodded. "But you may change your mind," he said.

"I won't. I know I won't," replied Matt stubbornly. "Not ever."

"That's all right, then," said Mr. Painter evenly. "I'll go along with whatever you want, Matt."

"Is Mom really ill? Will she have to go to the hospital?" Matt asked next.

"No, of course not. She's just worn out from everything," replied Mr. Painter.

"Are you sure? And is it my fault?" asked Matt.

"One hundred per cent sure, and of course it isn't your fault," said Mr. Painter. "We'll give her breakfast in bed tomorrow and I will cook the lunch. She'll be as good as new."

"It's been a terrible day, hasn't it?" asked Matt as they reached the woods.

"Life has its ups and downs. It wasn't meant to be perfect," replied Mr. Painter as he parked the car and both got out. "But don't give up, Matt. Never give up, not before the battle's lost, anyway."

The woods were dark and secret. Matt called, "Jessie, Jess, Jess, Jessie," over and over again until his voice gave up.

"We'll wait a bit. She may come yet," said Mr. Painter. "It didn't seem far in the car, but we're at least six miles from End Cottage," he explained. So they returned to the car and sat inside with the headlights on.

"I feel as though I'm hiding from something," Matt said. "A bit like a criminal. How could the robbers have hit Jessie? That's what I want to know. She's so sweet and harmless."

"I expect they were scared," said Mr. Painter. "People do dreadful things when they're scared. And anyway, maybe they were frightened and acted in self-defense."

"I couldn't hit any animal like that, I just couldn't," said Matt. "And who could be scared of Jessie?" asked Matt.

"You would hit something if it was trying to kill you," replied Mr. Painter. "It's a natural reaction."

"But Jessie wouldn't kill anyone," said Matt.

"They may not have hit her on purpose. It may have been an accident," said Mr. Painter.

"But Mrs. Charrington says she must have been hit with a spade," said Matt. "She says it's a wonder

Jessie isn't dead. That's what she said before you turned up at End Cottage."

"We may never know exactly what happened," said Mr. Painter.

They waited for half an hour, but spotted only a fox. It came out of the woods stealthily, looking this way and that. It blended into the landscape and then, like a phantom, slipped away in a sudden burst of moonlight.

Minutes later Matt said, "We had better go back now, Dad. Jessie isn't coming and I'm worried about Mom. I know fainting isn't a good thing, whatever you say, and she's never done it before."

"Have it your own way, Matt," said Mr. Painter, starting the engine of the car.

*   *   *   *   *

Jasper pulled Anne along. It was frighteningly dark until suddenly the moon appeared and lit up the bridleway, which was covered with hoofprints. Anne called several times, "Jessie! Come here, Jessie!"

Seeing her, birds flew out of trees and rabbits scuttled to their burrows. A hare disappeared across a newly plowed field, zigzagging wildly. Anne loved the moonlight. It seemed to make everything twice as beautiful, and somehow secret. London was lit at night by street lights, but it was never completely empty. There were always people—drunks on their way home, waiters, and endless taxis. It got quiet only from 3 a.m. to 5 a.m., but after that the milk trucks came in and the first bleary-eyed workers emerged on their way to early shifts. London in those early hours could be frightening, too. But here, the animals had taken over. Anne was the intruder.

The country sky was dark and speckled with stars, so that in spite of everything Anne was suddenly happy, and that made her feel guilty. Jasper was happy, too, though he longed to run ahead and chase the rabbits.

Being away from the Painters was almost a rest. The tensions had been almost too much for Anne.

At least Jessie has had a good life since she came into Matt's life, Anne thought. *If Matt and I hadn't rescued her from the stream, she would have had no life at all.*

Then she started to wonder how long it would take Matt to recover if he never saw Jessie again. How long would he wait for her to appear, her ears down and a loving look in her eyes? Would he ever recover from losing her? Unexpectedly, Anne began to cry again.

Jasper stopped to look at her. Then he licked her hand and Anne wished Matt could love Jasper as much as Jessie, though she knew he couldn't and probably never would.

At one point, she thought she heard someone calling, "Come back, Anne, you've gone far enough," but she wasn't sure, and she didn't want to go back. She didn't want to return until she had stopped crying.

But now Jasper was straining at his leash and looking ahead, and suddenly Anne could see the outline of a dog, walking in circles and sniffing at the ground. Her heart gave a great leap and she began to call, "Jessie, Jess, Jess, Jessie!" But the dog kept moving away from her and then she couldn't see it anymore. Still, she was sure now it was Jessie.

Anne started to call again, louder than ever, "Jessie! Jess, Jessie!"

But Jessie couldn't hear Anne because nothing was functioning normally—not her eyes, nor her ears, nor her nose. The blows she had been given had seen to that. So Jessie was blundering about, trying to find her bearings and failing. She wanted to go home, but she didn't know which way to go.

Anne continued to call, and sometimes she saw Jessie and sometimes she didn't. Suddenly, there were unexpected clouds in the sky. They looked like huge gray ships, which any moment now would obscure the moon.

Then Anne knew there was only one thing to do. She had to trust Jasper. He might disappear completely and become lost, too, but she had to take that risk. She unclipped the leash and said, "Find Jessie, Jasper. Bring her back. Fetch Jessie." And then she prayed, "God, make Jasper bring back Jessie, please, God."

She waited as the clouds obscured the moon, and for the second time she was afraid. First she was afraid that if she lost both dogs she would never be forgiven. Then she was afraid that if she left the path in search of the dogs she would never find her way back.

She switched on the flashlight she had been given, but its glow was hardly as bright as the eyes of the animals watching her. And now, without Jasper, the path was alien and eerie. She longed for welcoming voices and the lights of home, of any home.

Anne waited, and everything was suddenly very quiet and very black, and the moonlight was gone. Then she started to call, "Jasper? Where are you, Jasper?" Even her own voice frightened her, but it was so quiet when she stopped calling that she felt frightened again because she wasn't used to silence. London was rarely ever silent, neither day nor night. London never truly slept.

Then, without warning, there were things brushing against her legs and suddenly, Jasper and Jessie were there, licking her hands. She knelt on the path and put her arms around Jessie. "It's Anne," she cried. "Remember? We're going home."

She put the leash through Jessie's collar, while Jasper ran ahead, barking joyfully. Anne thought it was the best moment of her life. She couldn't see anything now because the flashlight had failed altogether. But her feet followed the path, step by step, and then suddenly she was running and calling out, "I've found her! I've found Jessie!"

Ten

MATT and his father were back at End Cottage. "Where's Anne?" asked Mr. Painter. "The moon's gone again and it's as black as ink outside. She isn't still out, is she?"

"I gave her a flashlight and she took the other dog," replied Guy Charrington. "She wasn't going far."

"We'll have to look for her. She could be in all sorts of trouble," shouted Mr. Painter. "What a day! First the car breaking down, then this. It's just too much."

Mrs. Painter had fallen asleep in a chair and Matt was biting what was left of his nails. His face was stained with tears.

Then they heard a voice calling, "I've found her! I've found Jessie!"

Matt rushed out of the house and down the bridleway. He stumbled over rocks and tree roots, shouting, "Anne, Anne! Where are you? Where's Jessie?" He wasn't tired anymore, but charged with new energy, which nothing could diminish. In moments, he was on his knees in front of Jessie, his hands gently touching her.

"Jasper found her," said Anne. "She was wandering about and couldn't hear me. I think she's gone deaf."

"Oh, Jessie," Matt said.

Mr. Painter picked Jessie up and carried her into End Cottage. They could all see how tired and out of sorts she was, more like a sleepwalker than a conscious dog.

Mrs. Painter woke up then. She smiled to see Jessie back, and to see her son so happy. "We can go home now, can't we?" she asked.

"Yes, we can take both cars," said Mr. Painter. "You drive one and me the other," he continued. "That is, if you're up to it, darling."

It was very late and they were all exhausted, but they had done what they set out to do and because of that they were thrilled.

Matt thanked the Charringtons several times. But then Jessie refused to get into the Volvo. As soon as she saw it, she trembled violently and crouched on the ground, whining. In the end, Matt and Jessie went with his father in the borrowed car, while Mrs. Painter, Anne, and Jasper got into the Volvo.

"We'll take it slow," said Matt's father. "I'll lead in case I break down again," he said.

Jessie whined whenever Matt touched her head. The clouds had left the sky and the moon was riding high and proud, turning the countryside into a fairy land. Matt felt choked with emotion and overcome by exhaustion. Soon, Jessie rested her head on his knees and slept.

The borrowed car thankfully didn't falter. After a few minutes, Matt fell asleep with his arms around

Jessie. When he woke up, he was at Willow Tree Farm. Jessie climbed out of the car like an old lady, but knowing she was home, she shook herself and raised her head, then licked Matt's hand. The back door wasn't locked and they found Uncle Eric asleep, with his head on the kitchen table.

Matt shook him awake. "We've got Jessie. We're home."

"By jove!" Uncle Eric cried. "But what happened to you? I've been calling all the hospitals. I thought there must have been an accident!" Uncle Eric had awakened with a start, and before he found his glasses and woke up properly he looked very old.

Then Mrs. Painter, Anne, and Jasper arrived in the kitchen. Aunt Lorraine woke up and came downstairs in a nightgown, her hair in rollers. They all looked at Jessie, especially Aunt Lorraine, who was a trained nurse and knew more about wounds than the rest of them put together. Her fingers were gentle and practiced as she felt Jessie's head. Matt waited nervously for her verdict.

"Will she be all right if her skull's cracked?" he asked fearfully, his small face looking pinched and tired. "Will she be able to hear again? Is she going blind? And what about her sense of smell?"

"I think she's going to be all right," Aunt Lorraine announced at last, getting to her feet. "She's very tired. She needs a long, quiet rest in her basket upstairs. She needs to sleep for hours and hours. She must not have any frights or walks, just peace. The wound doesn't need stitching and I don't think her skull's cracked, but her head is swollen and that affects everything. But if she isn't a little better in

24 hours, you must take her to the vet. Take her tomorrow evening if she hasn't made some progress and have her head X-rayed. But remember, rest is the best cure."

She looked at Matt. "No playing games with Jessie for several days, do you understand?"

And now Matt knew that it was the other Aunt Lorraine speaking, the one who had helped bring Uncle Eric back from the brink of death. He felt very grateful, so grateful that he rushed across to Aunt Lorraine and kissed her on the cheek.

"It was Anne who found her," said Mr. Painter. "If she hadn't gone up the bridlepath alone in the dark, we would still be without Jessie. It's as simple as that."

"I wasn't alone, and it was Jasper who brought her back," explained Anne. "Poor old Jasper, who always has a bad reputation. But he isn't bad and he isn't stupid. He's very, very clever—perhaps more clever than even Jessie."

"But not the same, not in the same way," said Matt.

"No. But I think he's wonderful," said Anne.

Jasper looked at her. His great, ungainly paws were on the kitchen floor and his strange, amber eyes looked up as if asking, "Are you really talking about me?"

Anne put her arms around Jasper's neck, burying her nose in his harsh coat. She turned to Mrs. Painter and asked, "Can he stay in tonight, please? I promise he'll behave. It's so hard for him to be shut away in the barn. And he isn't a puppy anymore. He's grown up, aren't you Jasper?"

And Jasper, who sometimes looked a little like

Jessie, but was so much bigger and had different eyes and a different tail, held up a paw to Anne.

"You know the saying—tell a dog he's bad and he'll live up to it," said Uncle Eric. "If we turn Jasper into a hero, he'll change, you just wait and see."

"By the way," said Aunt Lorraine, "I saw the late local news and the robbers have been caught and are in custody. The reporter said that the car and the robbers were found, but not the dog."

"Then I'll soon put that right," cried Mr. Painter, going to the telephone. "I'll call the police right away."

Mrs. Painter put on the kettle automatically, but they were all too tired for tea or coffee, or even hot chocolate. They were only fit for bed. Mrs. Painter kissed Matt and Anne goodnight. "No shop tomorrow. No shop ever again," she said.

Anne made Jasper a bed in the kitchen while Mr. Painter carried Jessie upstairs to Matt's room. Dawn wasn't far off. In just a few short hours, the rooster would begin to crow, announcing to the world that Willow Tree Farm belonged to him. Birds would begin singing, and another fine day would be under way.

Jessie lay down and slept in a way she hadn't been able to for more than 48 hours, a sleep of total exhaustion. And Matt slept, too, while Jasper fidgeted in the kitchen and tried to live up to Anne's expectations. Success did not come easily for Jasper, however. After a few hours he pushed open the sitting room door and climbed onto the sofa where Anne slept, and licked her face.

*   *   *   *   *

The robbers were all in custody now. They had been driving quite peacefully, until they spotted a road block ahead of them and a police car behind. They had given up without a fight. And though Darron worried about Jessie, the police wouldn't tell him anything. It wasn't until the next morning that a kindly policeman gave in and said to Darron, "The dog's all right. She's home. We heard the news late last night. So you're in luck this time."

Meanwhile, at Willow Tree Farm, the day was unfolding slowly. Uncle Eric and Aunt Lorraine were preparing to leave. Will was sitting on a stool in the kitchen, drinking coffee. Matt and Anne were still asleep, while Mr. Painter was mowing the lawn.

And Jessie was already recovering. She licked Matt's face while he slept, then put her head down and sighed. She was a little hungry, and curious about the voices she heard downstairs. While Matt slept, though, she would not leave him. She had been away from him long enough.

Mrs. Painter, still in her nightgown, said to Uncle Eric and Aunt Lorraine, "Come again soon, both of you. It's been lovely having you."

"Thank you," replied Aunt Lorraine. "Sorry to have to leave without saying good-bye to everyone, but we want to get away before the rush-hour traffic starts." And so they left, and slowly but surely life at Willow Tree Farm returned to normal.

The Volvo's inside was cleaned, and the borrowed car returned. But never again did Matt leave Jessie alone in the car, not summer, nor winter.

About the Author

CHRISTINE PULLEIN-THOMPSON has written children's stories for over 40 years. Born in Surrey, England, in 1930, she writes about animals surviving in the wild, raising ponies in the countryside, and hunting with woodland foxhounds.

At about age 15, Pullein-Thompson wrote her first book with her two sisters. Most of her stories have been about ponies.

Now she is director of a riding school. When she finds time, she writes children's books from her home in Suffolk, England, where she lives with her family, ponies, cats, dogs, and hens.

This is the third novel she has written about Jessie, a black Labrador.